Coastal Corpse

by

Rena Leith

A Cass Peake Cozy Mystery, Book 2

Coastal Corpse

Cover Art by *Debbie Taylor*

The Wild Rose Press, Inc.
PO Box 708
Adams Basin, NY 14410-0708
Visit us at www.thewildrosepress.com

Publishing History
First Mainstream Mystery Edition, 2019
Print ISBN 978-1-5092-2720-4
Digital ISBN 978-1-5092-2721-1

A Cass Peake Cozy Mystery, Book 2
Published in the United States of America

"In the spirit of the season—pun intended—I also thought Thor and I could have some fun scaring young children this Halloween if you don't mind. He is a black cat, after all, and he has a great set of pipes for long scary howls in the dark. You might get some trick-or-treaters this year now that this house is inhabited…" She paused for effect. "By the living. You'll probably get kids daring each other to approach the scary haunted house." She cackled. "It could be a whole boatload of fun!"

"As long as you don't hurt my cat."

Doris pouted. "I care about Thor, too." In the space between her words, she changed her clothing, materializing a cat suit. "He's my transportation."

As if on cue, Thor sauntered in from the living room and rubbed against her immaterial legs, purring. He looked up at her with adoring amber eyes.

"Did they celebrate Halloween back in the olden days when you were a flapper?" Jack finished loading the dishwasher and wiped his hands on the red kitchen towel.

Doris lifted her chin. "The Twenties aren't the 'olden days,' and of course we celebrated Halloween with grand costume parties." In rapid succession Doris' clothes changed through a series of ornate costumes from a golden-earringed gypsy to Marie Antoinette.

Jack raised an eyebrow. "Impressive."

"As long as you don't wander away with Thor while you're possessing him."

Doris pouted and vanished.

Also by Rena Leith

MURDER BEACH

Dedication

For my sisters: Susan and Tricia

Chapter 1

The light breeze riffled my hair as I squinted against the light glittering off the ever-shifting deep blue bay. September had been warm, but now a late October chill sharpened the air. The clear air carried voices down to me. I turned, expecting to see my brother Jack and his wife Gillian. They would be joining me for the first Halloween in my new house.

But they weren't there. Instead, several people chatted on my neighbor Dave's Krumpipe's deck. From a distance, it looked like three men and a woman. I recognized Dave. The quintessential surfer dude, he was medium height, muscular, towheaded, and lived to party up in San Francisco with his friends. I'd never known him to turn down an invitation to a party or a meal. He'd even eat my burned baking attempts.

An olive green jeep pulled into my yard. When Jack and Gillian got out and waved, I headed toward them.

"Cass!" Dave called.

I swung toward him and paused to wait. "Hi, Dave."

"Hey, Cass. I'd like you to meet my Aunt Amelia. She's visiting for a few days."

Amelia put her slender, beringed hand out. "Hi, Cass. Dave's told me so much about you."

I shook her hand. "Nice to meet you."

She had a firm grip for a small woman. Slightly shorter than I, her hair was chestnut brown like mine and her build slender, but the resemblance stopped there. Her eyes were vivid blue while mine were green with a small golden ring around the iris.

"And this is my cousin Niles. He's a doctor."

Niles was dark to Dave's light. His curly hair framed a high brow, and his eyes were so dark the pupils were almost invisible. He smiled lopsidedly, reminding me of Dave, and then held out his hand. "Not quite yet. I'm doing a residency at St. Agnes'."

"Pleased to meet you. Are you staying in the area?"

"Sharing an apartment with other residents, but I'll be visiting Dave from time to time. We're getting reacquainted. I've been busy with school."

I gestured between Amelia and Niles. "Mother and son?"

"Oh, no." Niles shook his head. "No, my mother died when I was a teenager, but Aunt Amelia has been like a mother to both of us. She runs the family trust."

The third man's cough was a hack. I wondered if he smoked.

Amelia raised an eyebrow. "My accountant Gerry Waverley. He's here to help redo some paperwork for us."

Gerry dipped his head as he stepped forward.

My first impression of him was that he was beige. Nothing about him stood out. I let go of his damp hand as quickly as I could.

"It's great to meet you all. I'm having a drop-in party on Halloween night. You're all invited. Many people will be in costumes, but don't let that stop you."

Jack and Gillian joined us. They were both tall, but

at six foot two my brother dwarfed me.

Amelia shook Jack's hand. "We were about to order some Chinese food. Would you like to eat with us at Dave's?"

She was as friendly as Dave. I'd only planned to order pizza, so her offer appealed to me. "What do you say, guys?"

"Sounds good to me." Jack answered quickly, and I guessed that he was hungry after their drive from Berkeley.

Gillian had opened her mouth, but she turned whatever her comment was going to be into a smile. My younger brother could be such a little boy sometimes. It was a good thing she loved him so much.

"Excellent!" Amelia said. "Let's say five for cocktails. It's been a long day."

"See you then." I rounded up Jack and Gillian, waved bye to Dave and his group, and pushed on up to the house to help with their luggage. I glanced at my watch. We had enough time to get them unpacked and talk for a bit before dinner.

"What have you got in this box?" I lugged a heavy cardboard box up to my door.

"Wait and see." Jack opened the door for me and dropped his suitcase down inside.

I set the box on my coffee table. Gillian followed us with her suitcase and beeped the car lock.

"My first Halloween here in my house and the first since the divorce." I spread my arms to encompass my beloved little Arts and Crafts bungalow by the sea. "This place was such a find! Bless you, Doris, wherever you are for chasing away other potential buyers and saving this cozy cottage for me!"

"Here! Here!" My little brother got a beer out of the fridge, raised it in salute, and took a deep swig. We'd resembled each other more when young before he shot up like a rocket. Now he was the tall, athletic one. He looked like an ad for a hiking magazine while I had become a suburban housewife, attending book clubs and experimenting with recipes. I shook myself. That hadn't been me even when I'd lived that life. It had been a role, but I was free now. Free to go hiking up in the redwoods if I felt like it.

Gillian, always empathetic, put an arm around my shoulder, yanking me out of my reverie. "Don't spoil your dinner. We're happy to be here to help you celebrate, Cass. I brought a few decorations from our stash in Berkeley. Plus..." Gillian tucked a blonde curl behind her right ear and reached into the box I'd set on the table to pull out a bottle. "Champagne!"

"So that's what was so heavy!"

Jack snatched it from her. "Let's put that in the fridge, Sweet Pea. My sis isn't fond of warm champagne."

"These days I'll take my champagne any way I can get it." I gazed around at the lovely woodwork that needed refinishing and the ceiling that needed repainting and wondered, not for the first time, if I'd erred in putting all my cash into this place a few months ago.

"Money problems already?" Jack frowned.

"I knew it would be tight when I used everything from my divorce to buy this place, but I also knew I wouldn't be able to get a mortgage without a job. I wanted a place of my own." I thought of the peeling burgundy and navy trim on the light blue exterior that would need painting soon.

"What about the web site business you started with Ricardo and Mia?" Gillian handed Jack the bottle.

"It's one client at a time as we get it up and running. I've already used the initial money from Brendan's Dust and Dreams bookstore site. I hope he'll buy the maintenance contract. We're kind of stuck with the design for Crystalline. Samantha's a tough customer. Her web site is more complex. It's going to take more time." I rubbed my bottom lip.

Gillian twisted her mouth. "How hard can it be to create a web site for a store that sells such beautiful jewelry?"

"The jewelry is easy, but Crystalline isn't only about jewelry. Samantha carries crystals and semi-precious gems of all sizes, shapes, and types. You've seen the ones set in wands and atop walking sticks or in wizard figurines."

Gillian raised an eyebrow and cocked her head to one side. "True, but if you focus on that, you could lose the gift and jewelry customers like me."

I glanced at my watch. "We'd better head over to Dave's."

Jack finished his beer and dropped the bottle in recycling as we trooped out the back door. The sun hadn't set yet, but by this time next week daylight savings would kick in and it would be dark at this hour. September had been warm, but daytime temps dropped to around 64 Fahrenheit these days.

Dave had the deck light on, and the door opened at our approach. "C'mon in!" Dave gave me a hug.

"Thanks for inviting us." I unzipped my jacket and hung it on his pronged metal coat rack. Dave's décor was eclectic. His lava light glowed and bubbled in the corner. A Moro pirate and his wife glowered down at us from the wall. I stopped myself. Who was to say that she wasn't also a pirate?

Dave had a small bamboo bar in the corner of his living room nearest the kitchen. He walked over to the bar, reached down, and grabbed a laminated drinks list that he set on the bar top. "Your pleasure."

I laughed. "I see you've done this before." I scanned the list while Dave reached into his mini-fridge, pulled out an IPA, opened the bottle, and handed it to Jack. "Hope you like pale ale."

"You read my mind." Jack took a deep swig.

I ran my finger down the list. "I'll have an Amaretto Sour."

Dave lifted the Amaretto and started mixing as Gillian looked over my shoulder at the list. I moved aside.

"Oh, a vodka gimlet please."

Dave placed my drink on a cocktail napkin in front of me. A moment later, Gillian had hers, garnished with a slice of lime and a sprig of mint.

"Dave, you're a genius."

Amelia coughed behind us. "I've set dinner up buffet style. Dave has such a collection of chairs and small tables. Seat yourselves anywhere." Amelia gestured at the table and plates of various Asian foods.

Jack was the first to oblige, snatching up a plate and loading it with Changsha chicken and prawns with walnuts. He headed toward a table for two, but Gillian nodded her head toward a couple of couches around a kidney-shaped coffee table. When he took the hint, she smiled at him. Though neither one saw me, I smiled, too.

I stood at the table, trying to make up my mind.

"Take a bit of everything. That's what I do." Amelia picked up a plate.

"It all looks so good." I took noodles, a spring roll, and garlic broccoli.

"Are you vegetarian?"

I shook my head, spearing a prawn. "Not really although I try periodically. Wave a slice of pepperoni pizza in front of me, and I cave."

Amelia laughed. "I ordered the Asian food to break the boys' pizza habit."

"Y'know, Clem's Clam Shack has a few healthy pizza choices although I've never been able to get Jack to go for the heavy veggie, light cheese, thin crust version."

"I can't imagine Dave going for that one, either." Amelia glanced over at Niles and Dave, who squabbled good-naturedly. "Like yin and yang those two."

"They certainly look very different. I didn't know Dave had any family, but then again I've only lived next door a few months."

"You and your brother bear a striking resemblance. It's nice to have family particularly in times of trouble." Amelia led the way to a small table near the lava lamp. "Dave told me a bit about the house you bought. Are you comfortable there?"

"To answer your question, yes, I am. I've upgraded a few things but I like the Arts and Crafts style with all the built-in cabinets and the beautiful dark woodwork, so I'm preserving much of the décor and furniture. I bought the place as is with all contents."

"Sounds like a great deal." She paused for a bite.

"You are aware that Dave paid the taxes on your house for a while."

"Yes." My stomach flipped. Was she staking a claim? "I thought it was odd that he'd do that, but he explained some of the house's backstory and told me he was afraid of what might happen to the place. He didn't want it torn down and replaced with a monster home that would block his view. Turns out anyone can pay the taxes." I couldn't tell her that a ghost chased owners away so all he had to do was keep it from falling into the government's hands. I quit babbling.

Amelia let me wait while she finished her Pad Thai.

Damn. She was good. Dave said she controlled their family trust. She'd be a tough negotiator.

A shiver of a smile touched her lips. "Relax. I'm not implying anything. I'm merely curious about your relationship with Dave." She sipped her tea.

"We're friends." I bit my lip.

She nodded. "Dave feels the same way. Does Dave do any work for you?"

I frowned. "No, but I'm sure he'd help out if I asked."

"So, no handyman work? No paying him cash under the table?"

"Again, no, but I'd certainly pay him if he did a job for me…and if I had the money to pay him."

Her eyebrows lifted. "I see."

I was sure she did and wanted to change the subject. "Do you live nearby?"

"No, I live in Seattle. But occasionally I rent a place down here that's close by. I like to keep an eye on my boys." She hesitated. "And there's an old friend who's taken a job down here… I may look him up." She glanced over at Jack and Gillian. "It's nice to connect with…family."

"Yes, it is." I wiped my mouth and put my napkin on my plate.

"Would you like more?"

"No, I'm through. Thank you so much for dinner, but we should be going. Jack and Gillian will be tired after their drive." I rose.

Gillian took my cue and, picking up her plate, also stood.

Amelia shook her head. "Leave your dishes where they are. The boys will clear. Thank you so much for coming."

Dave, always the good host, jumped up to get my jacket and hold it for me.

"Don't forget to come over for our Halloween party."

"Wouldn't miss it." Dave held the door for us.

"See you then!" I shivered as the night air hit me and scurried across what passed for Dave's yard. This close to the beach the soil was mostly sand.

"Did you lock the back door?" Jack asked.

"Nope."

Jack beat us in, but I was close on his heels. "How about some hot chocolate before bed?"

"Love some." Gillian swept her coat off and hung it up.

I searched the pantry for the chocolate. "I wanted to ask you guys to help me unload some Halloween decorations from my car, but it can wait until morning."

"Thank you," Jack said. "I wouldn't mind going to bed early. What did you think of Dave's family?"

"His aunt asked me if I'd paid him under the table for work around here. I thought that was a bit strange. Why didn't she ask him?" I took mugs out of the cabinet.

Gillian made her own cocoa, preferring less sugar than I liked. "Maybe she did and was verifying what he said. You know, checking up on him. I thought she was pretty sharp."

I microwaved a steaming mug and handed it to Jack. "Careful. It's hot."

He blew on the drink. "Niles seemed cool. Very different from Dave."

"No kidding! Definitely not a surfer."

After I warmed my own for a minute ten, we sat around the trestle table in the kitchen and enjoyed the chocolate silently for a few comfortable minutes.

Jack finished his first and pushed aside the mug. "Do me a favor and lock your doors tonight. I won't be able to sleep if you don't."

"Sure thing. I usually do, but we were only going over to Dave's."

Jack crinkled his nose. "There are crazies in this world. I want you to be safe." He placed his cup in the sink. "And to that end I'm going to check your whole house before we go to bed."

Gillian joined him. "I'll help."

"I'll lock the doors and clean up the kitchen."

Running the hot water, I squirted in some lemon detergent. In a jiff the cups were washed, dried, and returned to the cupboard. Then I went to the front and back doors and drove home the deadbolts.

Jack stepped down the circular stairs from my loft, leaving the light on up there. "All clear. We're heading for bed. 'Nite."

"Good night."

I turned on the hall nightlight, turned off the lights downstairs, and went up to my own cozy room. Thor, my big furry black cat, stretched then greeted me with a raspy meow. He gracefully jumped off the bed and padded downstairs to begin his nocturnal meanderings. Yawning, I changed into my cotton pajamas, switched off my bedside lamp, and curled under the covers.

Moonlight softly lit my bedroom as I drifted off to sleep.

Chapter 2

I had a lot to do today. Good thing I had help. I dressed quickly and drank a cup of coffee before Gillian joined me, every hair in place. I had no idea how she did it.

I yawned. "Morning."

She popped a pod into the coffee machine. "Jack'll be out in a few minutes. It takes him a while to get the blood flowing."

"Runs in the family." I yawned again.

Gillian pulled a face as she added half and half. "Did you get enough sleep?"

"I'm not sure what's wrong with me. Lack of oxygen. Want eggs?"

"Eggs would be great. I have some breathing exercises that might help." She sat down with her coffee.

Jack joined us. "Feels like a lazy day to me. Vacay."

"Don't even get in that mindset. We have loads to do today."

I whipped up a batch of scrambled eggs with cream cheese and dill. As I put the platter of eggs on the oak trestle table, someone rapped on the back door. I pushed the worn charcoal and ivory ticking café curtain aside to reveal Dave standing on the stoop.

"Does he have radar? He shows up whenever we're

eating." Gillian helped herself to the eggs.

"Food radar," I said as I opened the door. "C'mon in, Dave. Want some breakfast?"

"I can leave if I'm interrupting." But he made no move to go.

I smiled and shook my head. "No need. We have plenty."

"Here." Gillian handed Dave a plate.

He helped himself to the eggs and sat down next to Jack. I scanned the food on the table and added blueberry muffins I'd baked in anticipation of Jack and Gillian's visit along with a carafe of orange juice.

"Coffee, Dave?"

"No, thanks. I had several cups this morning already."

"I'm surprised you aren't having breakfast with your aunt and cousin." I served myself.

Dave pushed his eggs around his plate. "I needed to get out of there. Everyone was arguing. Loudly."

I exchanged a look with Gillian. Dave was not himself this morning. Jack perked up after eating.

"At least you have a trust fund, so things can't be too bad. My sister doesn't have a safety net with her money issues."

Dave turned to me. "I didn't know you had financial problems. Is your business doing okay?"

"It is, but we split the profits three ways, and we're just getting started. Things are a bit thin. We don't have many jobs lined up. You see my dilemma. I really need the income from getting Samantha's web site up and running."

"I might have a solution to your monetary dilemma and my own." Dave stopped pushing his eggs around and took a bite.

I paused with my muffin halfway to my lips. "You have monetary problems? What happened to your family trust?"

Dave looked away. "This idea I have…" He looked straight at me, his enthusiasm building. "It would involve you. Your house. I'd cut you in. It's a tour." He gestured with his hands. "You know about the legends round here. You've read Mina's books, and there are legends. We'd base the tour on them. We could end with your house and the treasure."

"Treasure?" I dropped what was left of my muffin.

"Maybe we could even dig it up ourselves."

"Dig?" I echoed.

"That would solve all our problems!"

I thought of the arguments that took place over in his cottage and wondered again what they'd been about. I snapped my fingers in front of his face. "Dave!"

He blinked. "What?"

"No, Dave. No tour of my house." I enunciated each word. "Especially no digging."

"But it would work." The tension of his energy raised the temperature in the room. "Doris could appear dressed like a flapper. Another legend is about the bootleggers—"

My heart beat fast as my stomach clenched. "Stop, Dave. No. No tour of my house."

He stared at me. "But why? It would solve both our problems."

"And create many more. I didn't move here to be an exhibit in a zoo." I pushed my plate away. Gillian started to rise as if to clear, but Jack pulled her back down and the two sat silently.

"But, Cass, I really need this. It's a great idea!" My usually laid-back surfer dude neighbor was so tense the veins in his neck stood out.

Gillian touched his arm. "Dave, please tell us what's going on. Maybe we can help."

He shook her hand off and turned back to me. "After all I've done for you? You can't do this one little thing for me? What harm would it do?"

I had never seen him so upset before. I would have bet that he was incapable of anger, yet here he was red in the face. Maybe even out of control. "Dave, what is it? What happened?"

"Never mind!" He stormed out the back door, letting it bang in the frame behind him.

I turned to Jack and Gillian, speechless.

Jack was the first to get his voice. "What was that about?"

Gillian shook her head. "Something must be terribly wrong. That is so unlike him."

I looked down at Dave's plate. "Very wrong indeed. I've never seen him abandon food before."

Jack snorted.

"This isn't funny." I wiped my mouth. "He's the beneficiary of a family trust. He's never needed money before. He's on good terms with the trust administrator, his aunt. We met her last night."

"Unless they all lied to us." Jack leaned forward. "Sis, you haven't lived here long enough to know what he needs or what he's like when he's stressed."

That was true enough. What did I really know about my neighbors? They knew more about me than I did about them because I was a blabbermouth and the newbie in the neighborhood. Or maybe I was so needy that I'd made assumptions about them because I wanted friends, people I could rely on, after my traumatic divorce from Phil. I snapped back to the present in time to see Gillian glower at Jack.

She turned to me. "You aren't at fault. Something weird is going on with Dave. We'll talk to him later. For now we'll help you get ready for Halloween, won't we, *Jack*?"

Jack stood up straight. "Yes, absolutely."

I smiled. I loved them so much. When he wasn't being an adolescent, Jack was my rock. "Thanks, guys. Since everyone in Las Lunas calls my place the haunted house, I thought I'd live up to it this Halloween, not with a legends tour, but with some old-fashioned fun."

Doris, my resident ghost, materialized next to the table and bent over the muffins, acting out smelling them even though we all knew she had no sense of smell.

"In the spirit of the season—pun intended—I also thought Thor and I could have some fun scaring young children this Halloween if you don't mind. He is a black cat, after all, and he has a great set of pipes for long scary howls in the dark. You might get some trick-or-treaters this year now that this house is inhabited…" She paused for effect. "By the living. You'll probably get kids daring each other to approach the scary haunted house." She cackled. "It could be a whole boatload of fun!"

"As long as you don't hurt my cat."

Doris pouted. "I care about Thor, too." In the space between her words, she changed her clothing, materializing a cat suit. "He's my transportation."

As if on cue, Thor sauntered in from the living

room and rubbed against her immaterial legs, purring. He looked up at her with adoring amber eyes.

"Did they celebrate Halloween back in the olden days when you were a flapper?" Jack finished loading the dishwasher and wiped his hands on the red kitchen towel.

Doris lifted her chin. "The Twenties aren't the 'olden days', and of course we celebrated Halloween with grand costume parties." In rapid succession Doris' clothes changed through a series of ornate costumes from a golden-earringed gypsy to Marie Antoinette.

Jack raised an eyebrow. "Impressive."

"As long as you don't wander away with Thor while you're possessing him."

Doris pouted and vanished.

"You guys can help me get the stuff I bought at the Halloween store out of the car." I stared at the mystery box Jack and Gillian brought with them from Berkeley and left on the coffee table yesterday. "What else have you got in there?"

Gillian tucked a strand of short, blonde hair behind her ear and opened the box. "We brought our costumes, and we have a bunch of these from previous years." She held up several pumpkin carving kits. "For some reason, we always think we'll turn into pumpkin artists, but it never happens. This year you'll keep us on the straight and narrow. We've also been gathering some things for you." She dug around in the container. "The days are getting shorter and chillier, so…" Gillian pulled a gray-green sweater with dolman sleeves out of the box. "Please get rid of that ratty old Kelly green one."

I took it from her and held it up, feeling the soft

wool. "This is gorgeous. I love it. Did you knit it?"

"I wish. So we can get rid of the old one?" Gillian leaned forward.

I hesitated.

"If you don't like the new one…"

I closed my eyes for a moment. "Okay. But that old sweater and I have gone through a lot together."

"It shows. Your turn. What've you got in your car?"

"Follow me." I led the way to my car and opened the trunk.

"Looks like you bought out the Halloween store."

"Jack, can you unload?" I handed Gillian a couple of bags from the back seat. "I want the house to look creepy. I've got cobwebs, skeletons, headstones for the beach, spiders, and a couple of cauldrons. I also bought a black candelabra with black metal bats and some orange votive candles." I hefted a box containing a glass punch bowl and ladle. "Can you get the door? This thing's heavy."

Gillian set the bags inside and held the door open. "It'll take us the rest of the day to strew all this stuff around and get the pumpkins carved."

"Let's hope there isn't a lot of wind overnight. These tombstones aren't very heavy." Jack had two in his arms.

"Stash those on the porch along with the cauldrons. They're for outside. I think we can throw stones in the cauldrons to weight them. We can add the dry ice later. There are a couple of small spotlights in one of the bags. You can help me decide where to aim them. I'll have to think about how to keep the headstones from blowing away."

"The headstones should have stakes to keep them in place. Oh, cool!" Jack held up the zombie arm stakes that I hadn't been able to resist buying.

"I thought you'd like those." Sometimes he was such an overgrown kid.

Gillian carried a few more tombstones up to the porch and went on inside. Jack and I finished getting everything up on the porch or in the house.

Jack plopped down on the couch, but I dumped a pile next to him. He groaned but sat up and peeled off price tags and wrappings.

"I'd like to try a couple of tombstones to see if they have stakes and how they work."

"Be my guest. I'll look for stones for the cauldrons. I hope it doesn't storm." I gazed out the window.

"None is predicted."

"I know. I'm a worrier."

Jack laughed. "You so aren't." He picked up one of the boxes and read the back. "When's high tide? We have to be careful where we place this stuff."

As I searched for rocks for the cauldrons, I peered over at Dave's house and wondered how he was doing.

We took a break around one, went into town to have lunch at Soupçon and picked up a few more things. Jack desperately wanted to buy a projector that threw a movie of a ghost up on a screen in front of a window, but I pointed out that we had a real live ghost who worked for free.

We finished as a ruddy sunset bloomed on the horizon and checked out our handiwork. Jack and Gillian erected a cluster of three tombstones near the front beach corner of the house. I'd half-filled the largest cauldron by the foot of the stairs. The purple bat lights and orange pumpkin lights cast spooky shadows over the front porch and lawn.

"Very cool." I dusted my hands off. "We're nearly set for Halloween tomorrow."

Jack nodded. "Now we only need to finish the jack-o-lanterns and place the spotlights."

As we went back inside, I cast a last glance toward Dave's.

Chapter 3

I woke the next morning to what sounded like a flock of woodpeckers.

Doris hovered over my bed. "Oh, good. You're awake. The cute cop you used to date is about to break down the door."

I groaned. "Doris, move. I don't want to experience your chilly ectoplasm until I've had my coffee."

"Hmmph!" She vanished.

I'd apologize later. I got up, grabbed my black silk brocade robe, and nearly fell down the circular stairs. I was halfway down when Jack opened the door.

George pushed past him and grabbed me. "Thank God you're all right!"

I tried to pry his hands off my arms. "Of course I'm all right. What's the matter with you?" Why was everyone behaving so strangely this Halloween? Bunch of lunatics. I'd have to check for a full moon.

He clutched me by the elbow and hauled me protesting out onto my front porch. He pointed at a crowd down on the beach.

I blinked against the early dawn light. "What time is it? What's going on?"

Thor chose that moment to let out a blood-curdling howl. George jumped and released me, giving me the chance to shield my eyes and squint toward the beach. I recognized the insignia on the van and the people taking pictures. The crowd was a crime scene unit. I groaned.

"Not another body!"

"This time it's a woman, and she bears a striking resemblance to you, down to the long chestnut hair."

An adrenaline chill flashed down the backs of my legs. "You're serious. This isn't a prank."

"Dead serious." He stared unblinkingly into my eyes, his lips a thin line.

My knees gave way, and I sagged against him. He put an arm around me and led me to the porch glider as I shivered and not just from the cold.

"Who? Why?" My lower lip quivered.

"I thought it was you at first, Cass. Similar build. Female. On your beach. Murder Beach. Then I noticed she was shorter, smaller. Do you understand what I'm saying?"

I nodded. "You thought it was me."

He shook his head. "I think it was supposed to be you." He closed his eyes and bent his head until it touched mine.

I pushed away. "No. Why would anyone want to kill me?"

"Look at your decorations. The tombstones. Anything missing?"

"We put them up last night. I don't really know."

"You're missing a tombstone. Either that or someone went out and bought one like yours, which is unlikely. Her body was laid out with a tombstone above her head. I think the killer is fond of the movies." His voice, soft and low, finally got through to me. "I'm asking you to think about it. The body of a woman who looks like you is lying on a stretch of beach in front of

22

your house, and someone has put a tombstone you own at her head."

"How do you know she was murdered?" His image blurred as my eyes filled with tears.

"I didn't say she was murdered."

"You implied it."

"We have to wait for the ME's report. But it's enough to provide you with some protection. You have to take this seriously until we know otherwise. Cass, are you listening to me?"

I stared at the scene on the beach, my mind racing. Who was she? Did someone really mistake her for me? Why would anyone want me dead?

Phil flashed through my mind, but even my ex wouldn't be stupid enough to risk life in prison—not when he was planning to marry his girlfriend.

Or would he? Even though it made no sense, the thought lingered.

I wasn't aware of Jack and Gillian until Jack spoke. "George, let us take her back inside now, okay? You've made your point."

George stood. "I have to be getting back. I'll be in touch later." He reached down to lift me up. "Stay inside until I call."

I let Jack and Gillian lead me back inside. "I locked the doors last night."

Jack sat me in a living room chair and lifted my feet onto a footstool. "I'm glad you locked the doors, but I wouldn't jump to the same conclusion George did."

"It shows how much he cares, though." Gillian wrapped a blanket around me and said, "We're fixing breakfast. You stay there."

I nodded, still seeing the scene on the beach in my mind's eye. Jack and Gillian murmured in the kitchen. Glass and metal clashed as they worked. It all washed over me. The smokey smell of bacon finally roused me. Rising somewhat shakily, I made my way to the kitchen.

Gillian waved a spatula at me. "Hey, didn't we tell you to stay put?"

I managed a weak smile. "When did I ever do what I was told?"

"Never. I can vouch for that." Jack set mugs of hot coffee on the kitchen table. "Sit. Drink. It's good for you."

I moved to stare out the kitchen window at the beach, but Jack blocked me. One glance at his set jaw and narrowed eyes and I parked myself at the table to warm my hands on the hot mug.

He relaxed and went back to frying eggs while Gillian buttered English muffins. My growling stomach reminded me I was hungry. I added sugar and half and half to my coffee and sipped until Jack set a plate in front of me. I looked up at him and smiled wanly.

Gillian parked herself opposite me. "How do you feel?"

"Better." I pushed the eggs around with my fork. "Do you think—?"

"No." She put two slices of bacon and a buttered muffin on my plate.

I picked up a piece of bacon and ate it. "Delicious. Thanks." I added pepper to my eggs and devoured them, hungrier than I expected to be.

Jack cleared his throat. "We have a lot to do today."

My eyes widened.

"Oh, yeah," he said. "You are carving a pumpkin. No ifs, ands, or buts. Do you have any candles we can put in them?"

I'd bought orange votives. Now what had I done with them? "I think I put the candles for the pumpkins in the pantry along with the wooden matches."

"Do you have a costume?" Gillian cleared dishes.

I narrowed my eyes, catching on. "Thanks for trying to distract me, but you don't think we should go ahead with the Halloween party, do you?"

"I think for now we should proceed normally. You've already invited people. Let's continue as though we're having company tonight. You invited George?" She rinsed the dishes and put them in the dishwasher.

I nodded. "And his partner Bill."

"Good. He knows about the party then, so we'll take our lead from him. If he says cancel, we will. Now, do you have a costume?" She dried her hands.

I took a deep breath. "Yes. Sort of a modified witch."

"Pumpkins?" Jack refilled my mug.

I sighed. "We have to pick them up. Sorry. Should have gotten them yesterday. I left it to the last moment."

Jack nodded and pursed his lips. "I'll go." He set his plate and mug in the sink.

I opened my mouth to protest, but Jack held up a finger, and I nodded. "Okay. There's a twenty in my jacket pocket on the hall tree."

"I think I can afford some pumpkins. We passed a farm stand on the way into town. They had piles of them." He slipped on his jacket, grabbed his car keys, and was out the door.

I stood. "I'm going to go get dressed."

"Need help?" Gillian asked as she rinsed Jack's dishes and added them to the dishwasher.

"Nope. I'm a big girl."

"Works for me." She smiled and sat back down to finish her coffee.

I climbed the stairs slowly, walked over to the window, and looked down. Below me the crime scene crew packed the last of their equipment into the van and drove off, taking my tombstone with them. The tide ebbed, and a few curious folk walked their dogs on the beach and looked up toward my place.

I donned a pair of jeans, my beige thermal sweatshirt against the morning chill, and slipped into my moccasins. Mornings on the Northern California coast in October could be chilly. The wind blew in off the slate gray ocean this morning, bringing its familiar salty tang. I joined Gillian downstairs. I would try very hard to wait for George to clue me in.

Gillian greeted me with another mug of coffee. "You may need this. It's going to be a stressful day and a long night, and we were up early."

I closed my eyes and smelled the fragrant cup. "Thanks." I sipped gingerly. "Jack?"

"Back in a few. Still getting the pumpkins." She smiled. "Probably picking through the whole pile."

I nodded and took another sip. "Probably George won't let us have the party."

"We'll be prepared in case he does. Besides, we need jack-o-lanterns for Halloween, anyway. Jack told me you used to love Halloween as a kid."

My eyes welled with tears. "But who'll want to

come when there's been a murder?"

Gillian set her own mug down and hugged me, careful not to spill my coffee. "We don't know if it is a murder. George'll let us know when he gets the autopsy results. It's going to be okay."

I had to ask. "Do you think he's right? Do you think someone's trying to kill me? Phil?"

"No, I think it's a coincidence. I think George cares about you, and he over-thought it. Besides, you gave Phil everything he wanted in the divorce. He'd be an idiot to kill you now."

I sniffled. "I need to find out."

"Why?" Gillian furrowed her brow.

"Because I won't feel safe again until I know. Gillian, I love this little house so close to the sea. I'm happy here. I like everyone I've met. I'm starting a company with two of the smartest kids I've ever met. It's a new start after Phil's betrayal. I don't ever want to feel like that again." I gritted my teeth. "I won't feel like that again."

"Take it easy, Cass. We don't know anything for sure. Let's get through today."

The front door opened, and I whirled around, ready to battle.

"A little help here?" Jack came in through the front door, trying to hang onto an armload of plump, orange pumpkins.

Gillian and I moved quickly to help him, bursting into giggles as pumpkins rolled everywhere.

Some of my tension ebbed. "Think you got enough?"

Jack scooped up a few tiny gourds. "I got these for the buffet table tonight."

I took several from him. "They're cute. We can use markers to put faces on some."

Jack dumped his burden on the table. "Are we doing standard jack-o-lantern faces or can we get creative?"

"The more creative, the merrier," Gillian held up a pencil sketch she'd been drawing of a bat flying near a full moon. "But if your imagination fails you, there are patterns in the back of the booklet."

"I take that as a challenge. Where's the newspaper?" Jack rolled up his sleeves. "What do you think? A ghost in honor of your haunted house?"

Doris rose up behind him, her arms extended above her head, her fingers curled into claws, and a positively evil expression on her face. I choked, and Gillian gasped.

Jack whirled around and spit beer. "Doris!" He did a full-body shiver. "Augh!"

Doris clasped her ghostly hands over her stomach, mimed laughter, and faded away.

"I'll clean up the spilt beer. Sorry, Cass." Jack grabbed the roll of paper towels we'd been using as napkins.

"It was worth it." Still laughing, I retrieved some newspapers from the recycle bin and spread them out on the trestle while Gillian opened the packages of carving tools. Doris had given me an idea for my pumpkin, and I used my doodling skills to sketch it out.

Two hours later, Jack opened his second beer and stepped back to admire his work. A credible Twenties' ghost, who bore a remarkable resemblance to Doris, adorned his pumpkin. It seems I was not the only one she inspired.

"Looks a bit like the silhouette of Nancy Drew on the endpapers of Mom's old blue hardback books," I said.

He took a long pull on the India pale ale. "It's an homage to Doris even though she nearly gave me a heart attack."

Doris reappeared. "Hmm. I approve." She changed her clothes to match the silhouette and turned toward my carving. "Nice cat. It is a cat?"

I cast a critical eye over my carving. What I'd intended to be a scary black cat like Thor with an arched back and hissing mouth instead looked like a pig with a furry tail.

Doris pursed her lips and regarded me with sympathy. "Nice try."

"Maybe no one will notice in the dark." I carried it to the porch.

Doris' laughter followed me out the door. I posed it at the top of the steps next to the railing and paused. While I stood looking out over the now-deserted beach, Dave and Niles came around the corner of the house. "Hey, Dave! Niles."

"Hey, Cass. Can we come in? It's freezing out here!"

"Follow me." I led the way in and called out, "Jack, Gillian, Dave's here with his cousin."

"Can he carve pumpkins?" Jack asked, brandishing a small, orange pumpkin saw.

Niles removed his jacket. "Is that a challenge?"

Jack spread his hands toward the table and pumpkins. "Be my guest."

Niles examined the remaining pumpkins. "This looks like a good one." He hefted a medium-sized pumpkin.

Jack spread more newspapers and handed him a package of tools. "Here you go."

"I'll need some coffee," Niles said.

"Dave, will you help me with the coffee?" Gillian asked.

"Make Jack a cup, too," I called. "He's already had a couple of beers."

Jack muttered something about pain-in-the-ass sisters, and Niles tried to hide his smile.

Dave and Gillian brought us steaming mugs.

"We can't stay long. We're expecting our aunt back this morning. She's handling some paperwork up in the City." Dave added sugar to his coffee.

"She left us to our own devices." Niles wiped his hands on a paper towel and sipped his coffee. "Always dangerous."

Dave took a sip. "But she's our favorite aunt, so it's always good to see her."

Niles closed his eyes and shook his head slightly. "Dave, she's our only aunt."

"That too." He grinned. "The trust business is taking a bit longer than she anticipated. She has a favorite AirBnB she stays at down the coast from here, but she's worried her time there will run out and she'll end up on my daybed."

"Where'd you stash the other guy?" Jack asked. "Is he local?"

Niles shook his head. "He's also from Seattle, but he's more conservative than Aunt Amelia. He's at a B&B north of here."

"The Moon Coast Inn?" I asked.

"That's the one," Dave said.

"That's a really nice B&B." I'd stayed at that inn when I first moved to Las Lunas, and I remembered Natalie Sandoval, the innkeeper well. I'd enjoyed my visit while we'd worked to make my new home habitable.

Dave seemed relaxed today, not as frenetic as yesterday. They appeared to have worked through their argument, whatever it had been about.

"Our party's tonight at dusk. C'mon over after you feed the ravening hordes of kids." Gillian leaned toward me. "Do we have enough food? Any idea how many will be coming?"

Given that neither Jack nor Gillian had mentioned the death on the beach, I decided to follow their lead. "I invited the neighbors, including you guys and Mina. Also, Ricardo, Mia, Sara, Samantha, and Brendan. Brendan might bring his renter. I told him that would be fine. My bungalow is small, but I think it'll hold everyone."

Gillian picked up a little orange net bag with a few chocolates in it. "I thought we could give these out as party favors. They could double as handouts for trick-or-treaters if we run out of candy."

"Hardly likely." Jack swept a hand over the side table that was rife with bowls of debagged candy.

Gillian returned the bag to the basket of favors. "We've got candy and party favors covered. Clem's Clam Shack verified the pizza order for the party. We have crudités and dip in the fridge. The usual cheese and crackers. Loads of drinks." Gillian waved a hand in the air, indicating all the Halloween decorations. "You're covered inside and out for atmosphere. Spooky and fun music on tap. Cackling skull."

"And we might have some additional jack-o-lanterns if Dave and Niles don't take theirs home."

Chapter 4

The moon cooperated and blossomed full over the bay, splashing silvery light across the breaking waves. A creeping mist hovered close to the ground, not enough to obscure the streets and hinder trick-or-treating but enough to set the mood for those who believed that the veil between the worlds thinned on this night.

Kids in fantastical costumes from space opera to fairy tales made their yearly candy pilgrimage among the houses as the sun went down. But I noticed that the younger children's parents, casting nervous glances my way, steered them away from my house and the beach area. That saddened me. But a smattering of teens and co-eds in elaborate costumes as inventive Victorians, romantic bloodsuckers, zombies, and dead pirates came by for treats. Jack and Gillian wore matching black leather jackets, jeans, and Doc Martens as they handed out candy to the small crowd.

Doris floated through, trying on a variety of costumes. My favorite was her black, high-waisted, suspendered tap dancing shorts and white shirt, her hair in finger waves softly framing her heart-shaped face.

"You do the best makeup, Doris." I told her before sampling the smoked oysters.

Doris pursed her lips, put her hands on her knees, and leaned over the hors d'oeuvres as if smelling them.

"These look dee-lish." Then she gazed at me and batted her eyelashes. "We can work on your makeup."

I laughed because my makeup was part of my vamp witch costume, including the penciled beauty mark on my cheek.

Gillian tried a smoked oyster. "The kid flow, such as it was, has diminished. Think you'll have adult guests soon?"

"I expect Brendan and his renter after the kids finish gathering treats from the porch of his old Victorian. Samantha shut her shop down early, so I expect her momentarily. Really curious about their costumes. Samantha's everyday clothes are a trip. Ricardo and Mia will drop by after they pick her mom up. I don't really think Mina will come although I invited her. She may drop in briefly. I don't anticipate too many of the neighbors because several of them have kids."

"George still coming?" She tried a scallop.

"We'll see. I invited him and Bill. Clem's should be delivering pizza any moment now, so I hope they show up soon."

Jack strolled up. "The swarm of candy-hungry vultures is thinning. Thor's sleeping on the porch swing. I deposited the bowl of candy on the table outside for any stragglers."

Someone knocked at the door.

Gillian left to answer it and returned moments later with half a dozen boxes of assorted pizzas. "Trestle table?"

"Yes, please. Help yourselves." I waved my wand in the air. "Pizza has arrived. Dig in!"

Jack let several more guests in, including Dave,

Niles, and two women I'd never seen before. He took them around, did some introductions, and gave the two women a snap tour of my place. He brought them over to me. "Meet your neighbors Theda and Maya. Theda is Carmen Miranda. Love the fruit hat. Maya's a mermaid with a strange resemblance to Esther Williams."

"Great costumes! Old movie buffs?"

Maya nodded vigorously. "We were film and digital media majors at UC Santa Cruz."

Theda was careful not to dislodge her bananas. "With a name like mine, would you expect anything else? Theda Bara? We love your witch, too."

"Thanks. It's a Harry Potter wand." I waved it careful not to put out anyone's eye.

"We recognize it. We're two houses down behind all the lilac bushes. You should come over for movie night."

"I'd love to. Pizza's in the kitchen along with drinks. Everything else is out here. I'm assuming you know more people than I do." I waved my wand around.

Maya laughed, displaying a dimple. "We've lived here for ages."

"Since graduating Santa Cruz," Theda added. "We didn't want to move back to Chicago."

"Too cold." Maya mock-shivered. "Lake effect snow."

"They don't call it the Windy City for nothing." Theda picked up a scallop. "These look yummy."

"I hope so. Let me know if you need anything." Out of the corner of my eye I saw George let himself in, followed by Bill. My heart skipped a beat.

George scanned the room for me. His gaze caught

mine, and he headed over. "Looks like the party's just getting started."

"You haven't missed much." I tapped him with my wand. "I want to talk to you."

"I thought you might." His soft lips brushed my forehead. "But we've put in a long day, and I plan to have a slice of that 'za I smelled when I walked in."

"You know where it is." As he and Bill headed for food, the front door opened again.

"Samantha!" I waved as she swept through the front door. Brendan followed in her wake with a slender, middle-aged man I assumed was his renter, the visiting professor. "Great outfit! Where'd you get it?"

"I had it made." She did a slow turn. "Victorian."

"I see that, but the tailoring is exquisite." I reached out to feel the beautiful fabric of the jacket and flipped the edge up to examine the stitching.

"Tailor in town. I'll email deets. She's fast and good."

"Thanks." I admired the teal worsted wool tailored to within an inch of its life. It wasn't my style, but the craftsmanship was undeniable and it fit Samantha's zaftig body perfectly.

As Gillian walked up to us, her eyes widened. "Love the hat."

A stuffed gray dove with folded wings perched atop a matching teal hat that tilted forward on her upswept hair.

I'd never seen Samantha's red-gold mane so confined. "Me, too. I'm blown away by the creativity in our little community."

Munching a slice of pizza, Brendan joined us, in a costume that added a foot to his height with a magnificent turban from which three feathers waved like some giant insect's antennae.

"Spectacular, Brendan!" I circled him admiring the orange silk robe that downplayed his portliness. "Is this a kimono? What are you?"

He chuckled. "It's a caftan, and I'm an Ottoman Turk." He held out an arm to display three-dimensional silk roses scattered all over the caftan and then held open the right side to display the blue fabric lining that also showed at the cuffs and lapels. "I made it myself."

Samantha cleared her throat and cast him a meaningful look.

Brendan's eyebrows peaked as he beseeched Samantha with his eyes. "With a little help. Under the caftan, I wear a long waistcoat of blue silk embroidered all over with flowers and vines and closed with a dozen frogs."

"It's so beautiful." Gillian touched the soft fabric. "I love the pants."

"Turkish trousers. They're five feet wide and held up by a drawstring. Very comfortable. The shoes are like bedroom slippers." As Brendan pulled his caftan aside to show off his slippers, the feathers of his turban swept the bottom of my chandelier.

"Careful. That's a huge turban."

"Thirty feet of muslin wrapped around my head."

"I'm so used to you in corduroy. This is such a change." I turned to the third person in their party. "But I see you brought someone in corduroy along with you."

The stranger laughed and held out his hand. "Hello, I'm Darius Democritus Stone, Visiting Professor of Comparative Literature and Folklore at Clouston

College. Pleased to meet you."

I shook his hand. "Likewise. And you came as a professor. Welcome to my home. That's quite a name."

"My parents argued over my name. My mother was a physicist and a fan of Democritus' atomic theory. My father was an architect. He admired Darius I, King of Persia, for changing the style of architecture of his empire." He smiled as his glasses slid down his nose. He pushed them back in place with his index finger. "But they could at least agree that Darius made a better first name."

"I agree. I hope you're enjoying staying at Brendan's. I'm new to the area myself."

"If you're new out here, have you heard anything about the Ohlone? I'm studying an offshoot that traces their ancestry to Coyote. Coyote is a trickster and a mediator between life and death. Some around here believe in were-coyotes."

"I hadn't heard that, but I'll tell my neighbor Dave. He wants to do a tour involving the local legends."

Darius' eyes narrowed. "Which neighbor would that be? I might want to talk to him."

I perused the room. "I don't see him, but he's the next house over along the beach. If you look out my back door, you can see his deck across the way."

"Thanks, I might do that."

After an awkward pause, I said, "Let me make sure all my guests are seen to."

"Of course." He tilted his head forward in a slight bow. "Do you mind if I wander around and have a look at your place?"

"No problem." I smiled. "When you're through, you'll have to try my scallops." I indicated the display of food. The noise in my house increased as new guests arrived.

"I'll do that now." He picked one up and moved off.

Brendan asked, "Have you heard anything further about the body on your beach?"

I nearly choked as his question brought back the images and emotions I'd been trying to suppress all day. "Word gets around fast. I thought we might avoid it during the party."

"It was on the news," Samantha said. "I'm so sorry it happened so close to you."

"I don't know any more than you do." I hoped George would appear but didn't see him right away. "I haven't had a chance to ask George what's going on."

Samantha and Brendan turned to look for him as well. The doorbell rang.

"I'll catch up with you later. I need to get that." Relieved to end that conversation, I let Mia and Ricardo in. They arrived in full steampunk gear. "Hi, guys. Love your boots, Mia."

She lifted her skirt to show me the gears and chains along the top. "Aren't they great? I finished them last night."

"They are, but I'm puzzled by your hat. It's a full-sized top hat. I thought it was supposed to be tiny. A fascinator."

She shrugged. "Everybody is wearing those. I found this in The Cabinet of Cali DeGaris and added a few of my own touches."

"Where?" I frowned. Not a place I'd heard of.

"New shop near campus," Ricardo said. "A bit of an homage to *The Cabinet of Dr. Caligari*, the 1920s'

German Expressionist film. Eclectic."

Theda joined us. "That's a great film! Did you see the remake from the Sixties? Robert Bloch wrote it. Glynis Johns stars."

"Theda, this is Ricardo and Mia. This is my neighbor Theda. Film major."

"Then you'll love Cali's shop. She was a film major. Loved the props, collected a bunch of stuff, and opened a shop. My favorite place to browse. You should come with us sometime."

"I definitely will," Theda said.

Doris chose that moment to appear, and I held my breath. Even though it was Halloween and people talked about ghosts, I wasn't sure they really wanted to meet one. But she looked as solid and alive as anyone else in the room. Her feet even touched the ground. She was dressed in a tasteful 1920s suit with a matching round hat and a single mink pelt around her neck. The beady eyes of the dead mink seemed to watch me as I stared at the narrow mouth biting its flank.

"Are you all right?" Samantha asked.

"I'm fine. Would you excuse me for a moment?" I moved as quickly as I could toward Doris. "Doris, that is completely creepy."

"What?"

"That thing around your neck."

"Isn't it great? The mouth has a clip in it." Doris sighed. "I wish I could apply pressure to the clip, but I have to revisualize it every time."

"Could you revisualize it gone?"

A glint in her eyes told me she felt mischievous, and I'd given her ammo to tease me with.

She swished her hips. "I think I'm growing very

fond of this creature."

I gave a little groan. When would I learn to keep my mouth shut? "Where's Thor?"

"Sleeping upstairs to avoid the crowd. Relax."

"Do me a favor and don't vanish in front of the guests. Go into a bedroom or something."

"Sure thing." She batted her eyelashes at me and moved off to flirt with someone else.

I rolled my eyes and followed Mia into the kitchen.

Samantha came over and winked at Mia. "Nice costume."

Mia cocked her head and raised an eyebrow at her. "Not so bad yourself." They both laughed, and Mia chose a pizza slice and headed for the living room.

Samantha watched her go.

I handed her a napkin. "What do you think of Brendan's boarder?"

"I like him. He listens to me and seems interested in my theories about Las Lunas. He thinks I should get a patent for my camera and has even offered to go with me on one of my ghost photography expeditions."

"Makes sense if he's into folklore." I'd been keeping an eye on George, waiting for him to be alone. "Excuse me." I found him. "Hey, there."

"Nice party." He smiled.

"You never answered my message about whether or not I should go ahead with it. I assume you didn't have any objections. Did you identify the body?"

"The victim is from out of town. I saw no reason why you shouldn't go ahead with your party. Odds are no one here knows her. No one has reported a missing person. We're still investigating, of course. But I can give you the information we've given the press. Her name is Amelia Stone." He frowned. "It's not like you to be behind on the news."

Two thoughts jolted together. I put my hand on his arm. "George, I met Dave's Aunt Amelia and his cousin Niles yesterday. Had dinner with them. I guess she resembles me, but I wouldn't have said she looks like me. Also, I met someone named Stone tonight. Brendan's boarder." I looked around for him. "Amelia's a very common name. It might not be her."

George's eyes widened and he tensed. "Really." He looked around the room. "Excuse me." He walked toward Brendan.

I was not about to be left out and dashed after him in time to hear George say, "I hear you have someone staying at your house."

"Why, yes." Brendan searched for his boarder. "Darius!"

Darius turned away from Samantha. "Yes?"

"There's someone I'd like you to meet. Professor Darius Stone, may I present Detective George Ho. Detective, this is my boarder Darius."

"Pleased to meet you." Darius held out his hand, and George shook it.

"Stone. We're investigating the recent death of someone named Stone."

Darius' smile faltered. "It's a common name." His hand shook slightly as he set his glass down. "Was the person male or female?"

"A woman about your age. Long chestnut hair. Slim."

Darius reached out for the table to steady himself. "Amelia."

George nodded. "What was your relationship to the

victim?"

Darius put his hand up to his eyes. "I was married to her. She was the love of my life."

"Were you in contact with her recently?" George kept his voice was very low.

I was pretty sure that no one other than the four of us heard him.

Samantha gasped, and I wanted to kick George.

Darius made a strangled sound. "I would never hurt her!"

"What brings you to Las Lunas?" George's voice was even and professional.

Darius straightened. "I'm a visiting professor at the college."

George nodded. "You knew she was here, didn't you?"

Darius hesitated. "I hoped…" His voice broke. "Can I see her?"

"You don't want to."

Darius went pale, swayed, and collapsed into a chair.

I dropped to my knees beside him. His skin was cold and clammy, and he breathed shallowly.

George squatted on the other side and took his pulse. He looked up at Bill. "Call the EMTs. I think he's going into shock."

I was torn between concern for Darius and anger at George for causing his distress. "Couldn't you have told him a bit more gently?"

George stood, took one more look around the room, and held a hand out to help me up, but he didn't answer my question.

"You wanted to see his reaction," I guessed.

"Sometimes it reveals the truth. Trust me."

"I do, but please don't bludgeon any more of my guests." I smiled to soften my words.

The hint of a smile raised the corners of his mouth.

After the ambulance left with George and Bill following in their car, the party was considerably quieter with people whispering to each other in corners. Word had gotten around. Theda and Maya said their goodbyes quickly but reinforced the invitation to come watch old movies with them.

"Cass," Brendan held Samantha's hand. "We hate to cut and run early, but we want to find out how Darius is doing."

"No problem. I completely understand. Please let me know what you find out."

Samantha squeezed my hand. "We enjoyed the party. It's not your fault."

"Thanks."

As the party dissipated, I closed the door behind the stragglers and surveyed the room. "Did you guys see Dave and Niles leave?"

Jack shook his head, but Gillian said, "They were in the kitchen a minute ago with Mia and Ricardo."

The three of us went into the kitchen. Dave, Niles, Mia, and Ricardo sat around the trestle table with drinks and food arguing about gaming. They all looked up as we walked in.

My mouth went dry. "Uh. Hi. Dave, have you heard from your aunt today?"

He looked at Niles, who shook his head. "No, but we didn't expect to. She's probably tired after the trip up to San Francisco. She knew about the party but wasn't planning to come, so we'll see her tomorrow.

Why?"

"Do you know a Darius Stone?" My voice faltered.

Dave frowned. "Uncle Darius? Aunt Amelia divorced him years ago. Why?"

Jack took over for me. "The police found a body on the beach this morning. Tonight we found out that they've identified it as your aunt, Amelia Stone. We didn't know who it was until a few minutes ago when Detective Ho told your uncle, who's a visiting professor at Clouston. When he heard, your uncle collapsed and is on the way to the hospital."

"No!" Niles got up. "C'mon, Dave. We have to go to the hospital." Niles slammed out the back door with Dave on his heels.

I sat down, my eyes filling with tears. "I can't believe she's dead."

"Did you know her?" Ricardo asked.

"Not really."

Gillian handed me a tissue.

"We met her last night and had dinner with her at Dave's. She was very nice. Dynamic."

"Now that you mention it, she didn't seem to be a good match with Darius, who seems much more timid. I can't imagine them together." I dabbed at my eyes. "It was so painful to watch as he heard what happened to his ex-wife."

"Ex-wife?" Gillian said.

I nodded. "That's what he said. They'd been married. He said she was the love of his life. I think that's why it hit him so hard."

"You realize that makes him the prime suspect if she was murdered, right?" Jack asked.

"He wouldn't," I said. "He loves her. Loved her.

Besides, George hasn't confirmed whether she was murdered or not."

But I was sure. Darius had nodded and started to say something. What was it? Oh, yes, he'd started to say he'd hoped something. I assumed he'd hoped to win her back, and that broke my heart.

Chapter 5

I woke up the morning after the party bright-eyed if not bushy-tailed, showered, dressed, and went down to the kitchen to make some coffee.

Jack walked in yawning, his hair sleep-tousled. "Gillian's taking a shower. She'll be out in a few minutes. What's for breakfast?"

"Coffee, juice, croissants with jam and butter. What do you feel like? Pancakes? Cold pizza?"

Gillian appeared, towel-drying her hair. "I need coffee."

My phone pinged. "It's from Ricardo. They'll be here within the hour." I texted back that it was fine.

Gillian fixed coffee for herself and Jack. "Is that about the web site for Crystalline?"

"I assume so." I stuck my phone in my pocket. "Okay. Breakfast?"

Gillian ran her fingers through her drying hair. "I think I'll help myself to a croissant with jam. Not really hungry after last night."

Jack already had his nose in the fridge. He emerged a moment later with a baggie of pizza slices. "I know what you mean. I feel kinda logy today."

I felt it, too. Lethargy that I didn't think was entirely due to party hangover. I took my coffee and went through the archway into the living room, slipped into the glider, and sighed. "I still have cleanup from the party." I looked over at the Art Deco figurines on the coffee table. "Are these the ones you think will sell?"

Gillian followed me with her coffee and perched on the end of the couch near my chair. "Yes, those are the ones from the built-in cabinet to the left of the fireplace. I haven't finished with the right. Tell me what you want to keep. I think they're all saleable and given that you're in need of money…"

I looked them over. "Good choices. While they're very delicate and pretty, I'm fine with selling them. The benefit of buying a house with contents included."

"Good. I've already done the research online. I'll write up descriptions, take pictures, and list them…later."

"Thanks, Gillian. I appreciate the help."

Jack emerged from the kitchen munching a slice of pizza. "Why don't I invite George over to help me get the car street legal?"

"Great idea, but does George even know about Doris' car? I'm not sure he does." I tried to remember if we'd ever mentioned finding Doris' old Packard convertible stashed in the rickety shed out back.

Jack shrugged. "Then he has a treat in store."

"Boys and their toys. I remember you sitting on the floor with those little toy trucks going 'vroom vroom.' You were so cute."

"Yeah, well, I remember you sitting next to me and running over my little trucks with your big truck!"

I chuckled at the memory. "Girls like their toys, too."

Gillian smiled. "Now, now, children. But Jack has a point. If Cass isn't going to make a move, I guess it's up to us."

"Guys, please. He knows how I feel."

Gillian raised an eyebrow. "Really? I didn't know you told him."

"I didn't. You know that."

"When did he develop the ability to read minds?"

"Gill—"

She held up her hand. "Cass, he can't read your mind. You have to open up to him. Be honest. Take a risk."

Someone rapped on the door. "I'll get it." Relieved to get out of answering her, I got up and let my visitors in.

"Hi, guys," Ricardo said, hanging his jacket on the coat rack.

"Grab a seat."

Mia said, "Can we set up at the table? It's easier with the laptops."

"Works for me. Anything to drink?"

"Coffee?" Ricardo said, and Mia nodded as she connected to my Wi-Fi and brought up the web site for Crystalline.

I looked over Mia's shoulder. "Those are gorgeous photos."

"Thanks," Ricardo said.

"You know you could make a career of photography."

"Thanks again, but I prefer design."

I nodded. "You're good at it. Does Samantha intend to keep a witchy theme or is this seasonal?"

"Seasonal," Mia said. "Unlike Brendan, Samantha wants her site to change periodically, and she's willing to pay extra for that maintenance."

"If we can get enough customers to buy maintenance, we can get a steady income stream going." Ricardo leaned back in his chair. "We're still discussing which cycles to use. Maybe seasonal or holidays. Her background is Catholic, but she's very New Age in her approach to her shop."

"True."

"So what do you think?" Mia asked.

"I think the site is brilliant. I also think we need to pin her down on how often we change the look. Halloween and Christmas are obvious, but Thanksgiving would be pushing it. We don't want to change it every month. Too much maintenance."

Mia said, "There's always the wheel of the year in the Celtic calendar. They divided the year up into parts like spokes on a wheel. I'm not sure that each of the festivals was a fire festival, but I can look that up."

I nodded. "It would provide a unifying theme for her site and still fit in with the combined community that we want to create by linking the sites using local myths and legends." As I said 'legends,' my memory of Dave's proposed legends tour washed over me, reminding me of Amelia's death. I leaned on the back of a chair.

Mia tilted her head. "Are you all right?"

"Not really. I think I'm having a delayed reaction to Dave's aunt's death."

"Sit down."

I pulled the chair out and sat.

"Do they know cause of death yet?"

I shook my head. "I don't think so, and I haven't turned on the TV today."

Ricardo pulled the computer over and did a quick

search for the Celtic calendar. "Here we go. Four major festivals in the Celtic calendar: Samhain on November first, Imbolc on February first, Beltane on May first, and Lughnasadh on August first. We could go with a hybrid because I'm quite sure she'll want to do Christmas. She does a lot of business at Christmas and Valentine's. Isn't there a solstice? What about Yule?"

"More research." Mia re-engaged. "We don't have to be exact. We just need to have internal logic that customers will understand, that Samantha will be okay with, and that we can handle from a business point of view."

"Samhain is Halloween. That's a good one to start with because most people already know the myths," I said. "If we launch soon, it's still valid."

Mia said, "Most other sites are into Christmas already, so we could do Yule."

"Good point. Are we agreed that we're ready to get Samantha's approval even though we don't have the holiday themes completely worked out yet?"

Ricardo said, "Any problem with my presenting it to her? I have a shift there later today."

"Works for me. What about you, Mia?"

She closed the laptop. "I'll do more research on Yule and gather info and motifs for each 'turn of the wheel.'" She stood and put her jacket back on. "I'm also following a possible lead for an update to the campus tour video. Might be another job for us."

"Sounds good. I'll run our plans by Samantha." Ricardo packed up the computer. "See you later." He and Mia left.

"I didn't want to interrupt," Gillian said. "But it sounds as though things are going well."

"Now I have to solve the problem of George and Doris." I frowned.

"You two can work that out. I plan to be nose-deep in grease in…" Jack looked at his watch, "about five minutes."

Gillian rolled her eyes. "Ever since he discovered Doris' old car he's been dying to get it running and street legal."

"Did you get hold of George yet? You could ask him about Darius while you're telling him about the car."

"Cass is right. Give him a call. Tell him about the car. Where's your cell?"

Jack dragged it out of his back pocket with two fingers and held it up.

Gillian raised her eyebrows and cocked her head at him.

Jack laughed. "Okay, Sweet Pea." He turned to me. "Cass, what's his number?"

I had to get my cell out of my pocket to look up George's number. "Nobody remembers phone numbers anymore." I read it to him.

He punched it in. "Hey, George. Bad time? Uh huh. What's happening with that? Do you think he did it? Uh huh. I know. Just thought I'd ask. Say, did I ever tell you about the car I found out in the shed behind Cass'? No, no. Not stolen. It's a 1920-something Packard convertible. Pretty good condition considering." He paused. "I'll be here." He shoved the phone back in his pocket. "He's off duty and on his way."

"What did he say about Darius?" Gillian asked.

"He was treated and released to Brendan. Niles and

Dave showed up at the hospital and talked to him. It's being treated as a suspicious death, but they are waiting on an autopsy. And I quote, 'Despite what you see on TV, they don't happen overnight.'"

"Thanks for trying, Jack. I'm going to change before we have more company." I headed up the circular stairs to my loft.

"Nothing wrong with your clothes," Jack called up after me and laughed.

In any other bungalow, the loft would have been the attic, but it was completely finished with a window at the top that overlooked the ocean and loads of under-eaves storage. After going through my entire wardrobe, I rejoined Gillian downstairs in time for Jack and George's return to the house.

"Great car!" George rubbed his hands together. "Let me know when you get it running. The paperwork shouldn't be too difficult. There's an application for historic cars. You knew there'd be paperwork. But the important things are that the car must be manufactured after 1922…"

Jack said, "Check."

"Be of historic interest."

"Check."

"And be at least twenty-five years old."

"Check."

"There are fees. You'll need to request historic plates. Also, you may face limitations on how far and where you can drive it, such as to car shows or within a couple hundred miles of home for pleasure. Do you plan to keep it here or take it home with you?"

To me, he sounded like a little kid with a new toy, and my heart warmed.

Jack couldn't stand still. "Can't believe it's in such good shape. I want to keep it that way. Nowhere to keep it in Berkeley. Okay if I keep it here, Cass?"

"No problem, but you'll have to do some work on that shed. It's an eyesore right now. Maybe George will help?"

"Happy to." George grinned. "While I'm here, I do have a question for you, Cass."

"Oh?"

"Do you know anything about a treasure associated with this house? Possibly associated with bootleggers?"

I knew I had a source in Doris, but I couldn't tell George that. "I think there was mention of it in some notes on the history of this house I got from Mia's mom. Her dad researched the house for a book. Why do you ask?"

"Do you have those notes? Do you mind if I wash my hands?" George asked.

"You know where the sink is. I'll look for the notes."

George went into the kitchen.

"Gillian, we moved stuff to get ready for Halloween. Do you know where the box with the manuscript is?" I asked.

"I think it's in the spare bedroom. I'll check." Gillian headed down the hall.

Jack frowned. "Didn't Dave mention digging up buried treasure when he talked to you about doing a legends tour?"

"Did he now?" George came back, wiping his hands on a paper towel. "Why does Dave want to do a legends tour?"

I exchanged a look with Jack. "He seems to be in

need of money. I need money, too. He thought we could work together to solve both of our financial problems."

"Would you happen to know if Dave inherits from his aunt?" George threw the paper towel in the trash.

My throat felt dry. "I believe both boys might inherit, but Dave did tell me once that he was the recipient of the trust at that time." I hesitated and George's eyes narrowed. I sighed. "Dave said his aunt was here to discuss trust business with himself and Niles. She brought her accountant with her."

"You're just telling me about the accountant now? Do you happen to know this accountant's name?" George glowered at me but made notes.

"Gerry Waverley."

"If you don't mind my asking," Jack said. "Why are you looking for buried treasure?"

George raised an eyebrow. "I hadn't thought about it being buried." He turned to me. "You know your house has a reputation for being haunted."

I bit my lip. "So I've been told." I really had to tell him about Doris soon before… I didn't even want to think about it.

"Your neighbor Mina has written several books about local legends and included a few about your house."

"Uh huh."

Gillian returned with a folder and handed it to George. He dumped the contents on my dining room table, separated out the photos, and quickly scanned the typed pages, pausing on two of them.

"This indicates that the woman who lived in this house might have had a fortune in gems secreted in this house or on the premises. She was a bootlegger's mistress."

The air vibrated. "George, first off, it's probably a treasure hunter's tale. They're rife out here in California. Second, if that information gets out, everyone and his brother's uncle will show up here with shovels. It's why I didn't want Dave to do his tour."

A flicker of a smile touched the corner of George's mouth. "Have you read Mina's books?"

My gaze cut to my built-in bookcase in the living room where I'd shelved Mina's ghost story books. "Not entirely. I've read a number of the essays and stories relating to ghosts."

"I'd say word is already out. Try doing a scan through her books for stories about treasure."

"Mina told us to read her stories," Gillian reminded me.

Jack nodded. "I thought she did it to promote her books."

George put the papers back in the folder. "She may have, but I'm sure all your neighbors know about your house and the treasure."

I slumped. "Great."

"Is this related to the woman's death?" Gillian asked.

"No idea. We follow up on all kinds of things." George smiled at her.

"You told Jack her death was suspicious. Is that true?" I asked.

"What do you think of Dave and his cousin?"

"Was it murder? Are they suspects?"

"Don't you know by now that with George everyone's a suspect?" Jack said.

I nodded. "Niles seems like a nice guy. A little tighter wound than Dave."

Jack rolled his eyes. "Everyone is tighter wound than Dave."

"Why do you ask, George?" Gillian asked.

George shrugged. "We took their info as a matter of course." George scrolled though his messages. "If you're through grilling me, I'd better get going."

"Hold it," I said. "Do you know how she died? I do have an interest given that you thought I was the intended victim…if she was a victim."

George pursed his lips. "She was."

I nodded. "Murdered."

Chapter 6

He nodded.

I swallowed hard. "Still think I was the intended victim?"

"No. If I did, I'd have been parked on your doorstep. Now that we know who she is and why she was here, we believe she was the intended victim."

I frowned. Why she was here? "How's Darius?"

His face went all iron jawed, but his soft voice belied his twitching face muscles. "He's recovering." George turned to Jack. "You'll have to get the car inspected and smogged. Do you have title to the car?"

Jack winced. "Actually, no. It came with the house. Cass bought the property and all its contents from a guy who moved somewhere like Kansas."

"I'm not sure he even knew the car was there," I said. "It didn't look as though anyone had even been in the shack since the Twenties."

"It might be a bit more hassle, but I'm sure you can trace ownership of the car, Cass, and establish yourself as the owner. Then you can sell the car to Jack…if you want to."

Jack turned pleading eyes to me. "You want to."

I smirked at him. "Maybe…"

"I'll never tease you again."

"Yeah, like that'll happen."

I watched George as he walked to his car and drove

off. "Did you notice he didn't tell us anything about Darius?"

"He didn't tell us much of anything," Gillian amended.

"I don't know why the two of you ever broke up," Jack said.

"I think it's fate that you moved to this particular town," Gillian said.

"Too late now," I said. "I can't afford to leave."

Jack picked up his keys and headed toward the door. "I need a few more things for the car and the stuff for the kitty door if you still want me to put one in."

I grimaced. "You know I'm short on cash, right?"

He stopped. "Haven't you gotten paid yet?"

"We did get a check from Brendan for the initial work. He also wants maintenance. He should be cutting us another in a few days. What I don't know is whether he will pay us in one chunk for the year or opt for payments, which we split three ways after expenses. Bookstores are narrow-margin businesses. We've already started on Samantha's web site."

"Given this is for the car. I'm paying…provided you sell it to me for a dollar." Jack looked at Gillian who nodded. "And the cat door is on us." He grabbed his jacket and left.

"I'll get the stuff listed for sale online. Some of it should bring in good money." Gillian asked, "Have you named the company yet?"

"We haven't decided. Ricardo likes RMC Ltd. Mia likes MRC Inc. I was going for something that gave a hint of what we do, such as 'Design for Living.'"

"But that's a movie title."

"I know. 'Icon' is taken, too. Dave suggested

'Larry, Moe, and Curly.'"

Gillian laughed so hard her eyes teared up. "Of course he did."

"Right now CaRiMia is under consideration. The only reason the first two letters of my name are first is because it's the best tonal combination. We'll submit several possibles to a lawyer who'll do the search, and that'll cost us. But that reminds me, I'm going to call Ricardo."

He picked up right away.

"Ricardo, I should have asked while you were here. Did we get a check from Brendan yet? I'm a bit tight, Christmas is coming, and the goose is anything but fat."

"Good news then. Brendan came through with one big check for the year. But we need more checks just like it. Tuition's due soon. I talked to Samantha, and she's changed her focus. More gems and jewelry now. But she is excited about the Celtic wheel cycles."

"That's great! We can move ahead faster."

"Your share will be deposited this afternoon. Give it a day or two." Ricardo hung up.

Gillian turned toward me, a red-checked kitchen towel in her hand. "Have you thought about putting in more modern windows? Don't know if you've noticed the night-time rattles and drafts. Maybe some shutters."

"Not a bad idea, but I'm afraid we'll have to do more business before I can make that kind of investment. And I want to keep the windows consistent with the period of the house."

When Jack returned, Gillian made him a cup of coffee.

"I'll help with the Halloween detritus after I drink this."

"It is a letdown removing the decorations. Any problem getting parts?"

"I thought there would be, but turns out there's a market for parts for these cars in California." He took a cookie. "Everyone's talking about the murder in town. Your name was mentioned, Cass."

"Me? Why?" I sat up straight.

"Everyone wonders why the murder took place in front of your house."

"Oh, for Pete's sake!"

"It's a small town. You're new and you live in the haunted house. Woo woo." Jack wiped his mouth with a napkin and got up. "I've got a kitty door to put in. The only reason I'm willing to do this is that you're so far from the road, and Doris agreed to be cat monitor when you're not home. If Thor wanders off, she can inhabit him and bring him back in through the cat door."

"She did?" I asked.

"I did." Doris materialized on the counter, her slender legs crossed.

Jack rummaged through my meager collection of tools in the pantry. He returned with a battered old drill. "It might get a bit noisy."

"Taking the hint," I said and joined Gillian in the living room where she played back the news recordings.

"I hate to be pushy, but you have to tell George about Doris."

I sighed. "I guess so since the other cops have told him my place is haunted."

Doris shimmered in. "I have no idea what you see in a guy who's afraid of ghosts."

"It isn't his fault," I said. "It's the way he was

raised in Hawaii. He's first generation American, but Hawaii is very different from the Mainland. He's heard mystical tales from his Chinese and his Hawaiian grandparents. He's caught between two worlds and both of them believe in the supernatural. I was fascinated by it when we dated in college but also jealous of his filial attachment to his family. Later I realized that included his ancestors. I caught him speaking to them as if they could hear him."

"Are you so sure they couldn't?" Doris asked.

"I'm not sure now, having met you." I laughed. "He always felt that spirits could follow him home. This isn't a case of him not believing that ghosts exist. He very much does believe that they exist, and it terrifies him. He might think that you'd follow him home, Doris."

"He's pretty cute. Maybe I will." She waggled her eyebrows lecherously.

I shook my head. "This is so not going to work."

"Does he still practice Qigong?"

"I didn't ask him. I assume so. He's in great shape." I stood. "I'm getting lemonade. Want some? It's made with the lemons from my lemon tree."

"Thanks. So far nothing on the news that we don't already know."

I nearly collided with Thor on the way to the fridge. "Bet I know what you want."

Thor sat up on his haunches and pawed the air.

"Gillian, you've gotta see this. Thor's learned a new trick."

Gillian came on the run. "Is he begging? Doris, are you in there?"

Doris materialized on the countertop. "No, but I

will take credit for teaching him."

Gillian snorted.

"Looks like he's asking for food." I addressed Thor. "I'm getting you tuna juice. That was so cool." I opened a can of tuna and rewarded him with his treat, poured lemonade for myself and Gillian, and rejoined her in the living room, handing her a glass. "Anything interesting?"

"Thanks." Gillian set the glass on a coaster. "They're asking the public for any information they might have. That's about it."

I frowned. "Maybe George was wrong and it is about me. I don't see any motive for her murder. Niles and Dave expected her."

"But Dave acted pretty strange when he proposed that tour. Something happened that made him think he'd need to make money quickly."

"Where's the accountant? Wouldn't he have information about what Amelia's trip was about?" I took a swig of my lemonade. "And what about Darius? Didn't he know his nephews were nearby? Why didn't he contact them if he wanted to reconnect with Amelia?"

Gillian sipped her lemonade. "Darius didn't strike me as someone who wanted to kill his ex-wife, but maybe he's a good actor."

"I don't think he's that good. He nearly collapsed. He doesn't look very strong, and while she was a small woman, she looked like she could handle herself."

Thor finished the liquid from the tuna can and was stretched out full length on his back on the rag rug by the back door. He looked like a very large, very hairy, dead black bug. I let him sleep.

Jack reheated some pizza and brought it over to the coffee table. "Keep an eye out for Thor."

Like clockwork, Thor's ears appeared on the other side of the table.

"He was napping in the kitchen a moment ago."

"He's like that. Maybe he and Dave are related the way they both home in on food." Jack grabbed him, flipped him onto his back, and rubbed his belly while Gillian swiped a piece.

"Hey!"

"It's my favorite," Gillian said. "Bacon, mushroom, and tomato with extra cheese. You don't mind, do you?" She batted her eyelashes at him, and he kissed her.

"I think I'll take George's advice and read more of Mina's books. Maybe have another look through Doris' diary. Speaking of which, Doris?"

Nothing. I wondered if she'd gone walkabout in some vagrant squirrel.

"Doris' diary?" Gillian asked.

I nodded. "I don't remember if I saw something in there or maybe it was only in the book notes on this house. Even if treasure were hidden here, it wouldn't have anything to do with Dave's aunt's murder."

"Speaking of which," Jack said. "Was there anything about the professor on the news?"

Gillian frowned. "Surprisingly, there really hasn't been much about him on the news."

"And not a mention of the accountant. What's up with that?" I opened one of Mina's books. "I could call Brendan."

"I disagree about the accountant. Probably cut and dried. Cops interviewed him and got what they needed." Jack hopped up. "Anyone need a beer?"

"Grab my cell off the counter while you're out there. Is he out of a job or does the trust employ him?"

He returned with a beer and tossed my cell into my lap.

I walked out onto the porch to make the call. The wind whipped the tips of the waves into a frothy meringue, so I paused to enjoy the view before dialing.

"Ricardo, hi. I wanted to know if you've heard anything about Brendan's boarder."

"Samantha likes everything we've done with the site, but she's very upset about the way the police have been acting toward Darius. At the moment the police have him at the station for questioning."

"Why? He seems so nice. I have trouble thinking of him as a murderer."

"He is a nice guy, but he's also her ex-husband."

I thought about Phil. Yeah, murdering him had momentarily flashed through my mind when I heard about his girlfriend. "I guess he would be the logical first suspect."

"Would you mind if we came back over? We have something we want to talk to you about together."

"The web site?"

"No, that'll be ready to go tomorrow. Samantha's up with our plan. It's something else and best discussed in person if you don't mind."

"Not at all. C'mon over."

"See you soon."

"Bye." I pocketed my phone.

Sunsets on the California coast are often spectacular with a golden richness of reds and oranges that darken to russet and brick before sliding into the sea. Jack joined me in time to see the last brilliant burst of color before the sun extinguished itself by diving into the sea.

"I love seeing the sun commit suicide every night."

"Morbid, sis. I thought you took physics in college?"

"I did, but I quickly discovered that my gifts lie with words, not differential equations. Oh, by the way, Ricardo and Mia are coming over briefly. Something they need to discuss in person."

"That's curious."

Thor banged on the door.

Startled, I turned around and opened the door. "Thoris?"

"Of course."

I still hadn't adapted to the weirdness of seeing Thor's mouth move and Doris' voice come out. "Where were you when I called you earlier?"

Ricardo and Mia pulled up in front and ran over to join us.

"Hi, guys, that was fast. What's up?"

"We were up the road when we called. We're on our way to my mom's for dinner." Ricardo put an arm around Mia's narrow waist. "How would you feel about taking some side jobs that aren't strictly web sites?"

I brightened. "Perfect! What do you have in mind?"

"Remember I mentioned a campus tour?"

"Yeah."

"I talked to several people this afternoon at school." Mia looked up at Ricardo. "We want to submit a bid. It'll happen soon, so we wanted to make sure you were on board before we did anything."

I looked at Mia and Ricardo's hopeful faces, liking their enthusiasm. And I really needed the money another job would bring even though it would be a stretch. "Oh, sure. Why not? What harm could it do?"

Chapter 7

After they left, we stayed outside to take down the Halloween decorations. The briny evening breeze blew in off the ocean, whipping my hair around.

"Where do you want us to put these?" Jack peered over an armload of gray plastic gravestones.

I shivered in the night air, and my thoughts went to Amelia Stone and Dave. Why had she been killed on my beach? This section of the shore was nicknamed Murder Beach because it had been a drop spot for bodies in the old rumrunner days. I didn't like that people were picking up the habit again.

And Dave. What had changed in his life to turn him from a fun-loving surfer dude into a nervous wreck who needed to make money fast? Well, I could identify with the make-money-fast part.

Jack said, "Cass?"

"Sorry. Just thinking about Dave. I need to talk to him. I have an uneasy feeling." I crossed my arms against the creeping chill.

"You could leave it alone."

"No, I can't."

He smiled. "I know. Why don't you go over to see how he's doing? Gillian and I can handle this."

I smiled at him gratefully.

"Tell him we're thinking about him, okay?" Gillian pulled a fake spider web off the azalea bush.

"I will. There might be some room under the eaves in my loft for this stuff, but it can wait until I get back. You could stack the grave stones on the porch and put the smaller items in the dining room for now."

"No problem." Gillian lifted the top off a pumpkin. "Maybe we can save some of these candles for next Halloween. We'll sort it out. Go."

"Thanks."

I headed off down the beach to Dave's. The tide was ebbing, and the sand was firm. His lights welcomed me as I climbed the few steps to his deck and knocked.

Dave looked up from the stack of papers he and Niles were looking through. He slid the patio door open. "C'mon in, Cass."

I stepped over the threshold. "Hi, guys. We're taking down the decorations, and I saw your lights on. It's rare to find Dave home in the evening. He's usually partying up in the city."

Niles smiled. "I'll have to get back to my residency soon, so we thought we'd better see what we can figure out." He gestured to the pile of paper. "And we have a lot to go over. We left a message for Gerry, but he hasn't gotten back to us. Aunt Amelia told us she had some serious business to discuss, but we didn't find anything specific in her stuff."

"I don't think we have all her papers. We should call the lawyer she went up to the City to see." Dave gestured to a chair. "Coffee?"

"Please." I sat. "So you have no idea what she wanted to talk to you guys about?"

Dave frowned. "Sort of. She was making changes to the trust. There are connected investments. She recently moved some money from one company to another. We signed papers for that transfer."

Niles shook his head. "She handled everything for us. We trusted her."

Dave brought me a mug and set sugar and cream on the end table next to me. "Each of us has a personal copy of the trust documents, so no mystery there. But we don't have copies of the proposed changes."

"We just don't know for sure what she planned to discuss with us. We think she wanted to change the structure of the beneficiaries and payouts, but we don't know for sure." Niles looked over at Dave. "Dave was worried. I have massive student loans, as you can imagine. The police have already talked to me about that."

"The cops are doing an autopsy, so they won't release her for burial until they've concluded their investigation," Dave said. "Who knows when that'll be. But when it's over, we'll at least find out if what she wanted to discuss was medical. You know, like cancer or something."

"Thanks." I fixed my coffee and stirred. "Maybe she wanted to discuss something simple like holiday plans with you guys. Do you usually get together at Christmas or Hanukah?"

"No, she indicated that this was trust business." Dave shook his head. "Our family is like a spider's web. Strung out all over. Loosely connected mess of cousins. The occasional dead bug wrapped in silk."

I opened my mouth and closed it again. I had no response to that.

Niles shrugged. "We don't usually get together for much of anything. No reunions. No holiday gatherings.

Not even birthdays. Mostly our family is comprised of overeducated and undersexed loners."

I almost choked on my coffee.

He held up his hand. "By that I mean that if you added up all the college degrees among the cousins and all the children, the degrees would be triple the number of kids."

Dave freshened Niles' cup. "Few siblings but quite a few cousins. Aunt Amelia had no children. Niles and I are Gram's only grandchildren, but her sister has three grans. So second cousins galore."

Niles picked up the story. "The elders don't last terribly long. Heart attack. Stroke. Skydiving accidents. But I'm sure that's more than you wanted to know."

I shook my head. "That's fascinating. And if I follow you, the two of you are the only surviving heirs of your side of the family. If something happens to the two of you, does another branch inherit?" I waved my finger between the two of them.

They exchanged a questioning look with each other.

Dave shrugged. "No idea. I don't have a will. You, Niles?"

Niles shook his head. "Never thought about it."

"The State of California will be happy to help you out by taking a chunk if you guys don't get wills, you know."

Dave nodded. "Yup. That's one of the things we need to look into. I'm assuming Aunt Amelia had a will. She administers the trust, but she has money in her own right." Dave gestured at some of the piles on the table. "This is everything I've collected. Niles brought his copy of the trust agreement and his correspondence with Aunt Amelia. We looked at the papers she had with her that were at the police station, but they kept them. We assume the accountant will fill us in if her visit was related to the trust. I honestly didn't pay attention to the name of the lawyer."

I had another thought. "Do you think she knew about her ex-husband teaching here?"

The guys exchanged a look.

Dave said, "I doubt it. We didn't know, and I live here. He didn't contact me."

"Nor me," Niles said.

"On the news—"

Niles cut me off. "We're not watching the news. It's really upsetting. We weren't that close, but the way she was killed…" He shook his head.

Dave got up and paced. "She was our mothers' sister. She loved us. Protected us."

As Dave rubbed the back of his neck, I felt more like an intruder. I put my mug down and rose. "I didn't mean to upset you, Dave. I'm right next door if you need anything."

He gave me a bear hug. "Thanks, Cass."

I closed the door behind me and walked to my cottage. The moon shone full and glistening. I slipped in my back door, happy to be home again. The warm glow from the living room drew me forward. Thor greeted me, rubbing against my ankles. Jack had turned on the gas fire, and the newly born flames flickered off the warm wood and green tile surround. Gillian sat on the edge of the couch taking pictures of the Deco figurines on the Stickley coffee table. She looked up as I entered, smiled, and nearly knocked over one of the statues. My joy bubbled up in my chest, and I laughed.

Having escorted me to the others, Thor settled into a ball in the glider and promptly fell asleep.

Gillian uploaded the pictures to her laptop and closed it. "Anyone hungry?"

"I'm not terribly hungry. Soup and sandwiches? Jack?"

"Works for me. How was Dave?"

"Really upset. They don't know much more than we do. He seemed very disturbed by the way she died."

"According to the news, bludgeoned and throat cut. Pretty brutal," Gillian said.

I shivered. "I'm going to turn on the exterior lights and lock the doors." I walked into the kitchen to flip on the lights. I looked back at Dave's cottage.

Gillian came up behind me. "Are they okay?"

"Not sure. Remember how worked up Dave was? Today they seem calmer. Subdued even, but they got more upset as I asked questions. I haven't known Niles long enough to read him, but Dave seems stunned and a bit lost. Turns out it's not a close-knit family, but it seems odd that they didn't know about Darius."

"I'm not sure I'd mention Jack if we were divorced or even know if he switched jobs."

"Are you divorcing me?" He walked up behind us and opened the fridge to pull out the cold cuts.

"If you're going to eavesdrop, do it for the whole conversation." Gillian reached for plates. "I'm only divorcing you if you don't get me a glass of that lovely Muscat."

"Your wish is my command." He grabbed the chilled bottle.

"I wish!"

"Ha ha." He handed her the bottle.

I got the glasses. "I'll have some, too. I need a little sweetness in my life right now."

"You should get George to take you up to Napa." Gillian poured me a glass and then one for herself.

"I'll have to get right on that." I took the glass and sipped.

"He seemed really concerned about you when they found the body."

"And yet he doesn't tell me a thing."

"Use your feminine wiles." Jack made himself a ham and cheese sandwich. "I could call him about the car again. Lure him over."

"What feminine wiles?" I laughed. "I know I shouldn't eat at night, but that sandwich looks good." I took a plate and two slices of rye. "And thanks for the offer, but I'm a grownup. I'll call him. I'm going to invite him to dinner. Are you two up for Cajun?"

Jack frowned and cocked his head. "You don't cook. The women in our family don't cook."

I raised an eyebrow at him. "What have you been eating since you got here?"

Jack counted items off on his fingers. "Let's see. Pizza. Sandwiches. Eating out."

"Dilled eggs? Scallops wrapped in bacon?" I said.

"Breakfast doesn't count."

"I can see you never want to eat again." Gillian reached for what was left of his sandwich.

"Hey! I made that myself."

"Settle, you two. I'm asking if you'll eat Cajun if I make it." I saw the mischief in Jack's eyes when he smiled, so I added hastily. "Without grabbing your throat and pretending you've been poisoned."

"You take all the fun out of life, sis."

Gillian swatted him lightly on the arm. "Of course we will."

"Let's take our food and dessert into the living room. Anything more on the news?" I carried my sandwich, wine glass, and a tin of shortbread into the other room.

Gillian brought the bottle of wine and sat next to Jack, wrapping up in the red crocheted afghan.

I sat in the glider Thor had vacated and turned on the reading lamp.

Gillian picked up the remote and checked the recorded news programs, selected one, and played it. When she fast-forwarded over the sports segment, Jack yelped. Gillian scowled at him. "You can watch the scores later. Focus. We want to know what the reporters found out if they're even covering the story."

I sat up straight. "George."

"What do you know? Our George is a TV star." Gillian rewound to catch the beginning of the story.

George was one of the people the reporter tried to interview. I could have told them he'd say "no comment."

The reporter narrated footage of my Halloween decorations and the beach that looked as though it had been shot with a cell phone.

"And so are you." Jack smirked.

My turn to glower at him. At least they hadn't tried to interview me.

My cell rang.

"Hey, George. I was going to call you later."

"I beat you to it."

"You did. What's up?"

"I thought you might like to go to dinner tomorrow

night. I'm off."

That stunned me, but I recovered quickly. "Better yet, why don't you come over here for dinner? It would mean putting up with my brother, but your reward would be some Cajun cooking." I smirked at Jack.

Jack rolled his eyes. I stuck out my tongue at him. Gillian put her hand over her mouth, but her shoulders shook.

"If my experimentation doesn't turn out well, you can take me out."

"I'm sure it will be great. What time?"

"Six-ish?"

"Terrific. See you then."

"Absolutely!" I flicked my cell off. "Ta da!"

Chapter 8

"I smell coffee." Jack was dressed in scuzzy clothes the next morning as he took a seat at my kitchen table.

"You do. Would you like a cup? And you need to wash those clothes. They're covered in greebies."

"Absolutely I'd like a cup. I'm wearing these old clothes again because the sealant on the garage should be set by now. I'm planning to paint today, and I don't want to mess up my good clothes. I'll wash these when I'm through with the job. I want the garage solid and weatherproofed before Gillian and I have to go back home. I thought she and I could take the car for a spin down the coast road to see if it's roadworthy. If so, I want to start the paperwork to get her registered as an historic car with license and insurance."

A disembodied cough echoed through the kitchen.

Jack looked up and ducked slightly.

Doris materialized on the counter. "You and Gillian are going for a drive?" She stared Jack down.

Jack looked away. "Morning, Doris. Would you like to join us? Given your ghostly limitations, I'm sure Thor wouldn't mind if you inhabited his body. I'd rather have 'Thoris' in the car instead of a random squirrel."

Doris crossed her legs and swung them, all smiles now. "Thanks. Love to!"

I suppressed a smile. "Don't hit anything before she's street legal." I put a mug of coffee in front of him. "I'm guessing you're going to have to prove you didn't steal the car given that you don't have a bill of sale. Can you even get insurance without title?"

"Don't worry. George is helping me. We'll have paperwork for you to sign so that I do have a bill of sale when I file. He wants a ride when she's legal." He smiled at Doris. "You can come for that one, too."

"Maybe you can get something out of him in exchange." I hinted.

Jack raised an eyebrow. "Doesn't getting him to hang out over here count?"

I kissed him on the top of his head, and he made a face.

Gillian joined us, yawning. "The sea air really makes me sleep soundly." She stretched. "Morning, Doris."

"You're not that far from the water in Berkeley."

"We're not this close. Can I help with breakfast?"

"No, it's all done. Crepes. I have no imagination, but they have eggs in them." I set jam, fresh strawberries, powdered sugar, butter, and syrup in front of them. Then I slipped a couple of crepes on each plate and put the plates in front of them. "I have no buckwheat flour to make savory ham and cheese. Sorry. Next time."

But Jack was already pouring syrup when there was a knock at the door.

I made a face at Jack. "Not Dave and Niles again!"

He looked out the back door. "Nope."

The knock sounded again at the front door, so I went to answer it. "C'mon in."

Doris vanished.

"Can't. We've got class. The dean approved our proposal but with a twist. They want augmented reality."

My confusion must have shown on my face because Mia smiled and shook her head. "Don't worry. We've got this. It's actually better and more fun and will show off our skills. We'll talk to you later."

"But—"

"We've got this." Ricardo repeated and they waved as they headed for Ricardo's car.

Still puzzled, I closed the door and went back to the kitchen. "We're using augmented reality."

"Cool," Jack said through a mouthful.

"You know what that is?"

"Of course."

We finished breakfast, cleaned up, and headed out to check my yard to make sure we'd gotten all the decorations cleaned up. Jack peeled off and went to the garage.

"Gillian, Dave said they still haven't heard from the accountant. I'm thinking of running up to the Moon Coast Inn. Want to come?"

She pursed her lips. "Let me see. Ride up the coast versus cleaning. Hmm. What do you think?"

I chuckled. "It's not that far up the coast, and we'll still have to clean and cook when we get back."

"Let's go!"

We stopped at the garage to let Jack know and drove up the coast a couple of miles. I pulled into the parking area behind the Inn.

As we walked to the front, Gillian paused looking around. "What a view! Every time I see a place like this, perched high on rocks with the ocean crashing below, all wood and window, I want to own a B&B."

I stopped next to her, looking out at the waves rolling in. "Not all B&Bs are like this. Some are farmhouses. Some are stately Victorians."

Gillian threw her arms wide. "One like this. Modern. Big porch. Huge windows."

"It's a lot of work."

"I know. You're a maid and a cook." She sighed. "But still…"

A voice behind us said, "But you get to meet and chat with some very interesting people."

We turned. Natalie Sandoval sat in a rocking chair on the porch. She wore a turquoise sweater that contrasted with her short, white hair.

I hastened to say, "We're not here for a room."

The corners of her sea-blue eyes crinkled. "I know, Cass. I expect you're all moved in by now."

"I didn't think you'd remember me." I walked up the stairs to the porch, followed by Gillian.

"How could I forget you? You were so stressed when you stayed here before your place was ready. Is this your sister?"

"Sister-in-law. Gillian, this is Natalie. Natalie, Gillian."

"Pleased to meet you, Gillian. Have a seat." Natalie nodded. "I saw your house on the news. Needs paint."

I opened my mouth to protest and then saw the twinkle in her eye. "Point taken. When I have more money."

We sat in two of the rockers. I rocked for a moment, trying to figure out how to broach the subject of Amelia's murder. "Do you mind if we ask you a couple of questions?"

"I'm guessing it's not about room rates or running an inn." She smiled.

"Do you have someone named Gerry Waverley staying here?"

Natalie smiled. "You know I wouldn't normally answer that question, but Mr. Waverley appears to have vacated the room early. The police have already been here, and I've been watching the news." She stood. "Let's go inside and have some tea. My shipment arrived today. Have you tried the white jasmine? It's delicious."

We followed her inside and sat in the parlor. She brought out a pot of tea and cups. "It needs to steep for a few minutes." She put one hand over the other. "My usual minimum is three nights."

I snapped up a cookie. "I remember you let me stay less than that."

"You were a special case." Natalie poured the fragrant tea. "Mr. Waverley's boss Amelia Stone stopped by and paid for the same room you had, and I left a late check-in packet in the mailbox for Mr. Waverley. Not unusual. I do it all the time."

"So you met her but didn't see him?" Gillian took a cookie.

Natalie shook her head. "The packet was gone in the morning. He didn't come down to breakfast, but that isn't strange." She poured Gillian a cup of tea.

"How did you know he'd gone?" I sipped my tea.

"He'd left a Do Not Disturb sign on his door, so the chambermaid left his room for last. Finally, she listened at the door. When she didn't hear anything, she came and got me. I knocked on the door and then used my key to enter. He was gone. Given that no one saw him, he had to have left in the wee hours."

"I don't remember you having any security cameras."

She pursued her lips. "Still don't. I was debating what to do when the police came and informed me of Amelia Stone's death and asked what room Mr. Waverley was occupying. They were surprised when I told them about his vanishing act. I asked them to return the keys if they found them, but I'll have another set made. I'm afraid there's nothing to see here."

"Did they tell you anything?" I set my empty cup back in the saucer.

She hesitated. "Not really."

"But?" I prompted.

"But Amelia was talkative while she was here."

I bit my tongue and kept quiet.

Natalie leaned forward in her chair. "She said she was here to talk to her boys."

Gillian nodded. "Dave and Niles."

"Yes." Natalie poured herself a cup. She added cream and sugar to hers.

I moved around in my seat. "And?"

"She seemed worried. She said there were irregularities in some account, a trust, I think." She sipped and added a touch more cream. "Someone had taken some money. Maybe one of the boys. She was upset and seemed disappointed. She was also worried about one of the boy's debts."

"Dave?"

"Hmm." She frowned. "No, the other one. Niles. She said he had a mountain of debt."

I finally took a cookie. "Did she say anything else?

More specific?"

Natalie shook her head. "I got the impression she was here to make adjustments between the two of them and finding the account irregularities was a shock because now she couldn't take care of both of them. Only one. She clearly loved them both. She talked about the mischief they got into together when they were young. One of them was more carefree."

"Dave."

"One was more serious."

"Niles."

"She said they were night and day. Her murder upset me. She seemed very kind and loving. A good aunt and a genuinely nice person."

Gillian drained her cup. "Not your typical murder victim."

Natalie peered into the pot. "Unless it was a random act of violence."

"It would almost have to be because she only came here occasionally to see Dave. Few people would have a motive to kill her, and even fewer knew she'd be here at this specific time." I stared at the earth-toned landscape on the wall behind the sofa. "That really narrows the field to Dave and Niles because Darius didn't know she'd be here."

Natalie warmed up Gillian's cup with a bit more tea. "Darius? I think she mentioned him."

"Her ex-husband."

She nodded. "I did see him on the news. They questioned him. I think she was going to meet with him." Natalie's brow creased. "But her demeanour wasn't that of a woman about to meet a lover. He seemed ill-suited to her."

"Really? We met him. I thought he was sweet."

She jerked her head back and then relaxed. "Well, you met him, and I only saw his picture on TV. Not to be unkind, but he appeared weaselly to me."

That surprised me. "We didn't think she knew he was here. Darius collapsed when he heard she was dead. I think he loved her very much, but you're right, he's not exactly the passionate lover type."

"Are you sure he didn't know she was coming?" She lifted the pot.

I put my hand over my cup. "Thanks, but we have to get back. Company for dinner, and I'm cooking." But I mulled over her words.

She set the pot down. "I'm glad you stopped by. It was nice to see you again. Come back any time." She smiled at Gillian. "I'd be happy to fill you in on innkeeping if you're interested."

Gillian cast one last glance around the spacious room. "Thanks. You have a lovely place here. The clean lines of the furniture and the nature hues of the fabrics are very much to my taste." She ran her hand over the nubby marine blue material of the couch.

"Thanks. I enjoyed every moment of decorating this place." She leaned toward us conspiratorially. "I knew I'd be spending a great deal of time in this room."

We waved goodbye as we crunched on the gravel.

Driving home, Gillian said, "I'll bet courthouses are haunted."

"What brought that on?"

"The emotions." She shook her head and looked out to sea. "The cases in court are often life and death. Murder."

I pulled into my yard. "A lot of cases that go to

court are really boring. C'mon, we should clean up a bit, but it's not like I have to impress George or anything."

Gillian laughed. "No, why ever would you want to do that?"

But she helped me as we spent the afternoon stowing Halloween decorations up in the loft under the eaves, shopping for supplies for dinner, cooking, and cleaning. Amazing how much sand gets tracked in so close to the beach. The sun was lowering on the horizon when George pulled up in front of my place. As I heard the car door slam, I peeked out the back door to check for lights at Dave's place. Nothing, but I didn't have time to give it much thought. I was at the door when George knocked.

The first thing I saw was the bouquet. "They're beautiful!" I took the large bunch of asters, lilies, and mums from him. "I'll put them in water." I went to the kitchen, set them on the counter by the sink, and pulled out a tall crystal vase.

"I'll take that." Gillian hung George's coat on the Arts and Crafts hall tree. "Would you like something to drink? I have water, tea, coffee, beer, wine sweet and dry, and if you trust me, I can give mixed drinks a shot."

"A beer would hit the spot." George followed me into the kitchen. "What are you doing?"

I thumbed through a guide to flowers I'd bought at the pet store. "I'm checking to make sure none of these is poisonous to cats."

"I hadn't thought of that. Can you put the vase up high?"

I set aside the guide. "I can do that. I don't want

dinner to get cold." I cut the ends off the orange and gold flowers and set the vase on the mantel.

Jack handed George a beer and got one for himself.

"Dinner smells delicious." George smiled.

"I hope it's as good as it smells." I went back into the kitchen and carried out a tray of crudités and dip and a platter of bacon-wrapped scallops and set them on the coffee table. "Starters."

Gillian followed with crackers, cheese, and mixed olives and cippolini onions.

Thor roused himself from his rug by the fireplace and stretched, arching his back. He advanced toward the scallops, and I shooed him away.

"He keeps me on my toes."

George reached down and rubbed Thor's ears until he purred. "He's certainly a beautiful cat."

"Thanks," Jack said. "He used to be mine. Had to give him up. He's a bit too large to hide. He's a bit of a chowhound. Wait until Cass serves the crawfish étouffeé. We may have to lock him in the bedroom."

"I'll put down some tuna juice. That should keep him occupied for a while. In the meantime, dinner's ready."

"What's this one?" Jack lifted the lid of a casserole.

"That's dirty rice with mini-chops. That little bowl is full of chopped scallions. And this one," I opened a second casserole, "is vegetarian red beans and rice. There's also a mixed salad with a small bowl of shredded cheeses on the side. I also have cornbread and lemonade. And any beer works with this cuisine, too. If you couldn't tell, I have a new cookbook." I glared at Jack. "I'm trying to live down the mistaken belief that women in my family don't cook."

"Beer works for me." Jack didn't meet my gaze as he moved around the table and took a chair.

"Do you need help with anything?" George asked.

I shook my head. "It's all ready. Find a seat." I pulled out a chair, and George took the one next to me.

Gillian moved across the table next to Jack. I poured a glass of lemonade and passed the pitcher to her.

Gillian put her napkin on her lap, helped herself to a nice portion of étouffée, and passed it. She took a bite and then made a small, happy sound. "This is so good."

"I enjoy cooking." I glared at Jack again. "It's really a case of being a plain cook and living alone. I don't usually pull together elaborate meals."

"Not even when you were married?" George took a piece of cornbread and didn't look at me.

I flashed back to my old life in Pleasanton for a moment. "I had important meals catered. Phil barbequed. Oldest trick in the book. Buy a man an elaborate grill and convince him that barbecue isn't really cooking, that it's a guy thing."

"Hey, some men cook," Jack protested. "Chefs."

"The days of only recognizing men as chefs is long gone." George passed the cornbread. "I'm pretty good at it, too. You should try my lumpia. I'll invite you all to my place for a reciprocal dinner. It'll be small and intimate because my tiny apartment is small and intimate."

"I remember when you made lumpia in college. I recently bought some from a street vendor in San Francisco, but they weren't like yours. They were hard like taquitos and didn't contain any vegetables. Yours were softer with shrimp and veggies inside."

"I'm glad you remember them so well. Remember the Kalua baboy?"

"Of course. I loved the crispy bits best."

"Baboy?" Jack helped himself to more étouffeé.

"Pig. Roasted for hours. Best done in an open pit, but you can also do it in an oven." He tilted his head and looked into the distance. "I suppose you could also do it in an instant pot, but I like slow roasting myself. Sets the flavor." He scooped up the last of his red beans and rice, wiped his mouth, and set his napkin down beside his plate.

"Dessert?" Gillian whipped the foil off the beignets and passed the plate.

I grabbed one and set it on my dessert plate. "Who wants coffee?" I stood and carried a few plates into the kitchen, put the coffee on, and took down some of the porcelain company cups.

Gillian set a few plates in the sink. "What's wrong?"

"I'm trying to figure out how to ask George what's going on with the murder."

"I was a bit surprised you didn't ask him outright while we were eating, but now's your chance. He really seems to like the beignet. Go. I'll bring the coffee out."

I returned to the table.

"Coffee?" Jack raised an eyebrow.

"Gillian's bringing it. George, Gillian and I were up at the Moon Coast Inn today. Is it true that Amelia planned to meet up with Darius?"

He sighed. "I really wish you'd quit playing Nancy Drew and leave it to the pros."

"Hunh uh. You're not getting away with changing

the subject." I said. "No way."

"We also know that you know more than you tell reporters." Jack took his cup from Gillian. "Thanks. We saw you on TV."

She set a cup next to George and one by me before tucking her skirt under her and sitting down. "So you think Darius did it?"

Jack got up to fetch his laptop.

George stared after him. "Was it something I said?"

"Jack handles data in spreadsheets, so he's going to input the data you're going to give us," I said.

Wiping his hands on his napkin, George chuckled. "So I'm giving you data?"

Jack opened his laptop and then the spreadsheet. "Of course. What did you find at the crime scene?"

"Other than the body?" George seemed more amused than annoyed.

"Uh. Yes." Jack looked up.

"Maybe you should start with a list of suspects." George sipped his coffee. "Let's see. Means. Motive. Opportunity. Stuff like that."

"Are you laughing at us?" I moved the plate of beignets out of his reach.

Jack leaned back and crossed his arms over his chest.

George raised his hands in front of him in a gesture of surrender. "No, no. Not laughing at you. You're so transparent. Don't ever pursue careers as spies." He laughed and shook his head. "Okay. I give up. What do you want to know?"

Jack hesitated and looked at me. I nodded. He opened a new spreadsheet and typed headers. "How was she murdered?"

"Her throat was slit, and we recently released the information that she was also bludgeoned. We have the scuba diving knife. She was hit with the hilt, and the blade slashed her throat."

I dragged my teeth over my bottom lip. "Does Darius go scuba diving? Doesn't seem like the type."

"There is no type for scuba diving. I used to watch the tourists in Hawaii when I was a kid." He paused. "But you're right. The knife belongs to Dave."

While I knew Dave and Niles must be suspects, it was a shock to hear that the murder weapon belonged to Dave.

Jack's fingers hovered over the keyboard, and he looked at George, his eyes wide. "Seriously?"

George waved his hand at him. "Go on. Type it in. We're releasing that info today."

Jack did as he was told and looked back up at George, voicing my own thought. "Dave's a suspect, too, or instead of Darius?"

"The body didn't appear to have been transported very far although there were some possible drag marks."

"So she wasn't killed on my beach?" That was a relief.

I jumped when Gillian poured some more wine in my glass and whispered, "Thought you could use this."

I looked down at the blood-red wine. "There was no blood on the beach. Was the body exsanguinated?"

George smiled, which made me slightly nervous. Usually, getting information from him was like shaving a cat, and I didn't want to jinx it by asking why he was cooperating with us.

"We're waiting for the pharmacology, but her throat was slashed post-mortem. No blood on the beach."

"Do you know where she was murdered?"

"Not yet."

Jack typed furiously.

"Wait a minute. What killed her?" I asked. "The beating?"

Gillian asked, "Do you know where she was killed?"

I looked at Gillian. "Not at the Moon Coast Inn?"

George shook his head. "No."

"Dave's?" My voice quavered. I so didn't want it to be true.

"Possibly. He does live nearby."

Jack paused. "I'm adding a column for the scene of the crime."

George smiled wickedly at me. "And you live nearby."

"You don't think—" I sputtered but realized he was teasing me.

"Would you care to elaborate on the suspects?" Gillian pushed the beignets toward George.

"I think you already have a pretty good idea who's on our list." George grabbed a beignet before she could snatch them away again.

Jack spoke the names out loud as he typed them in. "Dave. Niles. Darius. Unknown. Does that about cover it?"

"More or less." George licked the powdered sugar off his fingers before wiping his hands.

"Time of death?"

"Between 10 pm and 2 am."

"That's a pretty big range." Jack typed it in.

George nodded. "We'll narrow it down as we go."

I sipped my wine. "We know she'd gone up to San Francisco. She met people involved with trust business. Was she killed there?"

George smirked. "Really long drag marks."

"You won't tell us who she met?"

He took another beignet.

"When Gillian and I went to the Moon Coast Inn, we found out she rented a room for Gerry the accountant for three nights but he left early. Any idea where he is?"

"We're looking for him. What else did you find out?" George wiped his fingers on his napkin.

"Are you pumping me for information?" I had another thought. "What do you know about her business in the City?"

"Jack, you might want to add Gerry under suspects." George pointed at the laptop.

That stunned me. "Why? He was an employee. What did he stand to gain by her death? He lost his job unless the boys hire him."

"He seems to have vanished after our initial interview."

"Maybe he's another victim," Gillian said.

Jack typed. "Motive?"

George shrugged. "No idea at this point, but running doesn't make him look innocent. I'm beginning to think you don't like me for my charming personality but rather for what I know."

We all made little noises of insincere protest.

The corners of George's mouth twisted as he tried hard not to laugh, but the crinkles at the corners of his eyes gave him away.

I leaned back in my chair and crossed my arms. "When we were dating, I never gave you enough credit for a sense of humor."

"Here's something I'm not kidding about." George raised an eyebrow and tilted his head toward me. "People are saying that this was a nice, safe community before you moved here. They're saying that the murders started up after you arrived, Cass."

Chapter 9

I froze with the last bite of beignet halfway to my mouth.

"That's not fair," Gillian said. "This beach was called Murder Beach long before Cass moved in."

"Maybe so, but one body might be seen as misfortune. Two smacks of carelessness."

"Oscar Wilde? Really?" I said.

He shrugged. "Thought a touch of levity might help."

Suddenly the beignet was a rock in my stomach. I took a gulp of wine. The last thing I wanted in a new home was hostile neighbors.

Gillian asked, "We heard you're questioning Darius again. How is he?"

"Prime suspects are usually nervous. He's no exception, but Samantha and Brendan are looking after his interests. She invaded the station without advanced warning. Scared the crap out of some of the rookies. She got him a lawyer and took him back to Brendan's. She's nothing if not efficient." His voice was dry, but there was an underlying tone in it—admiration?

"Good for her." But I wondered how airtight his case was if Samantha could bail Darius out.

"So you think he's innocent?" George's voice was dead calm.

"I think he truly loved Amelia and was heartbroken

at her death." My voice was a bit harsher than I'd intended.

"And you think this because?"

"You saw him at my party! He moved here to be near her."

George nodded. "So none of that could have been a well-thought-out act?" George leaned back. "She doesn't live here. We checked, and she only visits Dave occasionally."

"But he might have moved here in hopes of seeing her."

"Cass, you're romanticizing Darius. It might be true that he moved here to reconnect with her, but it doesn't necessarily mean that it's a good thing." George's eyes narrowed. "Why don't you ask Niles about Darius' treatment of his ex-wife? See if he'll tell you why his aunt and uncle are divorced."

Jack tapped his laptop and brought our attention back to his spreadsheet.

George actually laughed. "Okay, what do we have?"

Had Darius been an abusive husband? How would I feel if Phil moved to Las Lunas?

Jack read the list. "Darius, Niles, Dave, Gerry, and Unknown."

"I vote for unknown," Gillian said as she rose and picked up a few plates.

That broke the spell, and George straightened up. "I should go. Thanks for dinner, Cass. It was delicious."

"Whoa. Hold it. What motive does Darius have?"

"Seriously, Cass? How do you feel about your ex?" George raised an eyebrow at me.

It was as if he'd read my thoughts. "I wouldn't

faint the way Darius did if someone told me Phil had died. I'd dance a jig, but I'm also not planning to kill him."

"But you wouldn't mind if someone else did."

"I'm not saying that. I don't wish anyone dead."

"But do you get my drift that some people do? Some people actually kill or hire it out. I think everyone's capable of murder."

"Seriously? That's an awful way to look at people."

Gillian paused on her way to the kitchen. "So you think Cass is capable of murder?"

I looked from her to George, really wanting to know what he'd say.

"Yes. Yes, I think she could kill someone. Under the right circumstances."

Gillian nodded slightly as if confirming something to herself.

I caught a glimmer out of the corner of my eye. Doris perched on my circular staircase in her seafoam green dress. She shook her head.

George turned, following my gaze. I held my breath, but he didn't appear to see her. He turned back to me, frowning.

In the ensuing silence, he got up. "I don't suppose it would do any good to tell you to let us do our jobs."

"None at all."

"Didn't think so. Never could get you to listen to reason. Take care of yourselves. Lock the doors."

"What's that supposed to mean?" But there was no answer as I closed the door behind him.

Jack exhaled. "Sorry, sis."

I nodded. "That didn't go quite as planned. Not a

romantic evening, but we did get some information."

Gillian finished clearing. "Let's not let that be the last event of the day. How about calling Brendan? Maybe there's something we can do to help."

"Great idea." Jack closed the computer. "I've started a bunch of things but haven't finished any of them. I have a couple more touches on the cat door, and then I'll have completed one job. I'll do that while you call Brendan." He got up.

"I guess I'm calling Brendan." I slipped my jacket on, picked up my cell, and went out onto the porch to avoid the sound of the drill in the kitchen. "Hey, Brendan. How's it going?"

His voice sounded strained. "I'm worried about Darius, but I'm also worried about Samantha. Darius is so upset about Amelia's death that it's all he can talk about, and that's bringing back memories of Samantha's dead fiancé. They go back and forth." He lowered his voice. "It's driving me crazy. There's nothing I can do to help either of them."

"Would it help if we invited Darius over here for a change of scenery? You and Samantha are also invited, of course."

"I think it's a great idea, but he should go alone. They need to be separated. Otherwise, they're both headed into a downward spiral." He paused.

"But?"

"But I don't know if I can get him to leave the house. He didn't get out of his pajamas today."

"Does he need to see a therapist?"

"Probably, but I don't think I can get him to do that, either. And I'm not really in a position to insist."

"Brendan, not that I think he did it, but can you or

Samantha alibi Darius for the time when Amelia was killed?"

"Do you know what time she was killed?"

"Between 10 pm and 2 am."

Brendan sighed. "I'm pretty sure he was asleep in his room. I shut things down, lock up, and go to bed around ten. I have a security system because I have some pretty valuable things here, but it isn't a sophisticated one. No cameras. Darius knows the code. He went upstairs after dinner. We ate together. But as I told the police, I can't be one hundred percent certain that he stayed there. He says he went to bed around ten-thirty. I can only say that I thought I heard him as I went to bed around ten fifteen."

"Thanks, Brendan. I don't want to think he did it, either."

"I don't think he had anything to do with it. He's deeply mourning. I'm worried about his effect on Samantha. If you could get him to come over, I could take her out somewhere and try to raise her spirits."

"Sounds like a plan. Do you have his number? I could invite him over here for lunch on the pretext of picking his brains for some ideas on using folklore for Samantha's web site. That way he'd be using his expertise to help Samantha. If they're bonding, he should be willing to do that for her."

"Do you seriously have something he could help you with?"

"Absolutely. We're developing some mythological themes for her web site so that we can change the site for each season, hit the major gift-giving holidays, but provide enough tie-ins that the site seems familiar but slightly different each time, to keep up customer interest. He could check our research or suggest other myths."

"That's a great idea, Cass! Thanks so much. I'll talk to him and give you a call back." He hung up before I could suggest that I should call Darius.

Oh, well. I stuffed my phone in my pocket and enjoyed the play of moonlight over the gentle waves on the bay. It was so quiet that I heard the lapping waves and the rustle of leaves. Something small squeaked in the distance. I breathed deeply and went back inside.

****

Brendan was as good as his word and apparently quite persuasive. He and Samantha dropped Darius off at my bungalow at noon the next day. They begged off my offer of lunch and waved as they drove off.

"C'mon in, Darius." Only now did I think that meeting here might be uncomfortable for him. As I caught his quick glance toward the beach, I hurried him inside. "We've got lunch all ready. I hope you don't mind me picking your brains."

"No, no, not at all. Anything I can do. Brendan and Samantha have been so good to me. Samantha's a force of nature."

"Hi, Darius." Gillian took his jacket and hung it up. "She's a character. We're set up in the dining room." She gestured toward the table. "Jack, bring Cass' computer here."

Jack joined us, carrying the computer. "Hi, Darius. Did Brendan explain that my sister and a couple of students at Clouston have started a company?"

"Yes, and he showed me the web site you developed for him. Very Brendan."

"Have a seat." I gestured toward the table.

"Samantha's will be very different reflective of her store and personality. I can show you what we're thinking about."

Darius sat as Jack handed me my computer.

"What can I get you to drink? Wine, beer, lemonade, iced tea, water? We might still have some soda from…" Gillian caught herself before mentioning the Halloween party.

Darius smiled slightly. "It's okay. Amelia's death…" His voice broke. "I never stop thinking about it."

"I'm so sorry." Gillian clenched her hands together.

Darius shook his head. "Don't worry about it. Nothing you or I could say would change anything. Iced tea would be terrific. Thanks."

Gillian slunk off toward the kitchen.

I opened the laptop. Jack's spreadsheet was still on the screen.

Darius blanched. "What is that?"

"Sorry about that." I closed the spreadsheet program and clicked to the demo file for Samantha's web site. "This is what we have so far." I clicked through the pages. "I'm afraid we're looking for Celtic cycles without any real knowledge. We want the look and feel to be similar from page to page. Icons. Color schemes. But we don't want to make it too busy or confuse clients. We want to create atmosphere but put the emphasis on her products to enhance sales. Do you get what we're going for?"

He nodded. "I think so, and I think I can help."

Gillian set his tea next to his plate.

"Thanks." He reached for his glass while reading

the computer screen, raised it to his lips, and took a sip without looking at it. He set it back down and pointed. "For example, you've got a mix of time periods and cultures that would annoy any Celtophile. You can achieve a better effect by choosing one span from one culture that has all the elements you want and then do some tweaking based on logical projection. Here, let me show you what I mean." He reached for the mouse.

An hour later Gillian had to reheat the soup, but we finally had lunch. Darius became more engaged with our project and less wrapped up in his sorrow. Such a nice, gentle man. I really couldn't see him killing his ex-wife. I tried to imagine him enraged, but no. What did George see that I didn't? What had Niles told him? Or had George shifted his focus to Dave? Or worse, was George stringing me along, trying to distract me?

Gillian set a plate of brownies on the table and helped herself to one. "Professor, obviously you teach folklore, but do you believe it? Years ago I read Frazer's *Golden Bough*. The way he wrote was as if he believed what he was writing."

Darius wiped his mouth, laid the napkin next to his plate, and leaned back in his chair. "I couldn't make up my mind between anthropology and literature as a student, so I combined them. Story fascinates me. When you're dealing with myths, stories, and human behavior, you use inductive reasoning to come to a conclusion that may be overturned later by someone with a better-honed hypothesis. But unlike some of my colleagues in Ed Psych, I believe that human behavior is fuzzy. Not always predictable or quantifiable. This is also the tack Frazer took."

Gillian nodded. "Yes, but do you believe it?"

"Believe?" He shrugged. "Everyone has a story. Even those who don't believe in what they can't see have stories. I have my myths and journeys. I guess I would say that to some extent I believe most myths and legends as having some toehold in reality. 'There are more things in heaven and earth, Horatio, than are dreamt of in your philosophy.'"

"You were interested in my house because of the stories about it. Is it because you believe in ghosts?"

Someone else was very interested in our conversation. The air shimmered.

Darius stared directly at the space Doris invisibly inhabited. I was curious about how some people seemed to be able to sense her. He shivered as he turned back to us.

"I'm always interested in new stories, aren't you? We're meaning-making beings. By that I mean that we try to explain everything we experience to make sense of it. I think many people believe and think they've seen—"

"Darius," I said. "We're all trying to say that the rumors are true. I have a ghost."

He raised an eyebrow over his glasses and looked down his nose.

I hesitated. Maybe this wasn't such a good idea. We'd only wanted to distract him. "You know what? Never mind." I got up and started to clear.

Gillian placed a hand on my arm, stalling me. Then she addressed Darius. "Would you believe if you saw her? Talked to her?"

"I usually believe the evidence of my eyes and inductive reasoning. Once all other possible answers have been eliminated..." His voice trailed off as Doris joined us.

She had flair. She'd dressed in the lovely seafoam green dress I'd first seen her in. Doris died in the Twenties, and today, despite her ability to change her appearance at will, her choice of clothes and makeup were appropriate for the age in which she died. Her dark hair in its classic bob framed a pale, heart-shaped face containing large, blue eyes under arched, pencil-thin brows and a red bow mouth. When I'd first seen her, she looked like a living being. Today her image wasn't quite as clear. The blue of her eyes and the red of her lips were more like suggestions of color. She was a bit ghostly.

"Holy Toledo!" Darius froze, eyes wide.

"Pleased ta meetcha." Doris dropped a curtsy.

Then she faded out and faded back in dressed like Katherine Hepburn in *The Philadelphia Story,* trousers and all. She left Darius in no doubt that she was supernatural. She also left him completely speechless. Darius did the only thing a modern person could do. He looked around for the means we used to create her.

Jack laughed. "She's not a projection. I thought what you do now, but she's real. Or… Not exactly real. Well, yes, real just not alive. She's—"

Gillian kissed him on the cheek. "We get it, Jack. Professor, we all had the reaction you're having when we first met her. But we've traced her history. It tracks."

Darius pursed his lips. "This is quite a good trick."

In for a penny, in for a pound. I cut to the chase. "Doris, can you show him Thoris?"

Doris vanished, and a moment later my cat did handsprings across the living room. Then he stood on his hind legs and walked over to Darius. Thoris said, "Happy to meet you, Professor."

If Darius was nonplussed to find himself talking to a cat, he gave no sign. "Your lips don't match your words."

"You're an educated man. Have you ever seen a high degree of articulation in a cat's lips?" Thoris said with a definite lisp.

Darius frowned and poked Thoris in the mouth. Thoris bit him but didn't leave. He started to poke her again, and Thoris said, "Next time I'll bite it off."

Both Darius' eyebrows rose. "No need to get tetchy." He looked up at me. "How does this work?"

"Beats me. I was as surprised as you are. She can possess animals."

He looked back down at Thoris, squinting behind his glasses. "Does everyone know about her?"

"Oh no. Ricardo and Mia know. However, Brendan and Samantha don't. Mina, one of my neighbors, knew before I even moved in. She was at the original séance that raised Doris."

Gillian stepped into the conversation. "The short version is that Doris' mother owned this house. She had another daughter who inherited it. Both mother and daughter were writers. The daughter's writing group had a séance with other locals to raise her mother's ghost as a muse for their group. They raised Doris instead, and she's been here ever since. I have no idea about the mechanics of it all. If I hadn't met Doris, I wouldn't have believed it was possible."

Darius' brow creased. "The Twenties. The other daughter. Is she still alive? Could we talk to her?"

I shook my head. "Francine, Doris' much younger

half sister, has dementia. I'm afraid that door has closed."

He nodded. "That's a shame."

I wondered if he meant her dementia or his inability to question her. "You don't have to believe any of this is real. Feel free to think it's a trick or projection. I merely wanted—"

Darius interrupted me. "If you are a ghost, do all people who die become ghosts? Is Amelia…?" He wiped at the corner of his eye.

I'd wondered the same thing. "I have no idea. Doris has been on the beach and—"

But Doris rematerialized outside of Thor, who shook himself, howled, and stalked off, vocalizing under his breath. "I haven't looked lately."

"Oh. Uh." I took a sip of my tea to buy time because Darius frowned at me. He was pretty sharp on the uptake.

"I've been living in Brendan's house long enough to know that Samantha's searching for the ghost of her dead fiancé, and she said she was looking on your beach."

"So that's what she's doing!" Jack said.

Gillian added, "We knew she was trying to film something supernatural around town and around Cass' cottage, but she never explained what she was looking for."

"And we knew her fiancé had died, but…" With a sinking feeling, I suddenly understood. "Oh. He died on my beach."

Darius nodded.

"Well, that explains a lot. You understand that we have no idea how any of this works. Even Doris isn't sure. Thanks for letting us know about Samantha."

"She and I talk. There's been a lot of tragedy in her life. I don't know everything, but I do know she's alone…except for Brendan now." He turned to Doris. "Why are you here?"

She shrugged, hands raised. "Beats me, honey. I thought I'd go into the light when I found out how I was murdered but no dice."

"Have you ever seen Samantha's fiancé on the beach?" His eyebrows knit together in a hopeful look.

Doris shook her head. "Nope. Sorry."

He took a deep breath, held it a moment, and exhaled slowly. "Did you see the ghost of my Amelia?"

She cocked her head. "Didn't look. Sorry."

His voice softened. "Would you look for me now? Please?"

She nodded. "Of course." And vanished.

Chapter 10

I tensed up, waiting for her return. We all were on high alert.

Doris popped back in. "Come out slowly and quietly. I can only barely see her. She's repeating. I don't know if I can get her attention."

Darius leapt up, but Jack grabbed his arm. "Slowly."

He fought for a moment, but Jack was much taller, younger, and stronger than he was. He gained control of himself, his mouth a tight line, straightened his lapels, and nodded at Jack. We all moved carefully and quietly toward the door. Gillian opened it, and we tiptoed out onto the porch and squinted down toward the beach.

At first I saw nothing. Then there was something. I strained to see a shift in the light. A shimmer. It was like an animated GIF or a very short video. Just a few seconds of movement. I tried to relax and see the image.

Darius cried out, "Amelia!"

The little replay didn't change or acknowledge him, and he emitted a frustrated cry.

Doris held up a hand to us to stay where we were as she drifted down to the beach. I couldn't tell what she was doing, but it looked like she was synchronizing with the replay. Doris became vague, a shadow of herself, and started repeating with the image.

Suddenly, she sort of fell out of the little movie and lurched back toward us, dragging the wet, iridescent image of a woman with her. The woman staggered, held out her hand toward us, and collapsed.

"Amelia!" Darius rushed toward her hazy form, dropping to his knees and trying to pick her up. His fingers passed through her and raked the sand.

Amelia vanished.

"Don't try to touch her!" Doris vanished and returned with her again, picking her up without effort and carrying her into the house.

Jack gave Darius a hand up as he shivered from the close contact with Amelia's incorporeal form.

"Thank you. I-I…"

I took Darius' arm. "Let's go back in the house before the neighbors think we're throwing a party."

Darius nodded and let me lead him back into the house.

I directed him to a chair. "I know this must be a bit of a shock. It certainly was for me when I first met Doris."

Doris laid Amelia's inert ghostly form on the couch facing the fireplace.

"She seemed to know me." His eyebrows drew together.

But that wasn't what I saw. She'd made eye contact with me. "I wish I could tell you more, but we're learning from Doris."

Doris solidified. "I don't remember my death. So don't expect too much when she comes back."

"Comes back?" Darius' voice broke.

Doris pursed her lips. "I don't know exactly how to describe it, but I'm not here or conscious all the time.

I'm still sorting it out. If it works the same for all ghosts, Amelia will come back to consciousness, and then we can talk to her. I can also be present but unseen. Kind of like controlling the volume."

"Doris can fine tune how solid she appears," I said. "And what she wears."

"And her makeup," Gillian added. "Are you all right?"

"No," Darius said. "Not sure I ever will be again. I feel as insubstantial as Amelia looks."

"Shock." Jack handed him a beer.

"Not sure alcohol is a good—" My caution was too late.

Darius took a deep swig and sighed. "Okay."

Amelia sat up. "Where am I?"

Darius hurried over to the couch and tried again to touch her.

As his hands passed through her, she wavered and her midsection vanished. She glanced down at herself and gasped. "What's wrong with me?"

He drew his hands back abruptly at the cold clamminess. "It'll be all right."

"Am-am I dead?" She tried to touch him, but he recoiled in fear.

"Okay, enough!" Doris stepped forward, hands on hips. "Stop! Amelia, yes, you are dead. Stop touching him! You'll learn to use that later."

I knew she meant as a weapon against the living. It had been very effective in getting me to cooperate with her.

"Darius, Amelia is dead. She's a ghost. Stop trying to hold her. You can't, and it will just creep you out. Both of you, back away. Now!"

They did as they were told and scooted to opposite ends of the couch.

"Okay. Amelia, what do you remember?" Doris' voice was gentle.

I held my breath, hoping we had an eyewitness to her murder.

She gazed at Darius. "I was waiting for you to come home from teaching." She shook her head. "No, that's not right. It's Christmas and... No. Your mother complained about my cooking. You stalked me?" Her eyes widened. "Did you kill me?"

"No, no. Of course not. I still love you, Amelia, but someone did kill you. Do you remember who?" He reached toward her but hastily pulled his arm back when Doris took a step forward.

"I came to see the boys." She frowned.

"Yes. Dave and Niles. About the trust." I tried to encourage her memory.

But she frowned again. "The trust. Something wasn't right."

"Do you remember what wasn't right?"

She frowned and turned back to Darius. "Why did you leave me?"

"Amelia, you left me."

"I did?" Her expression was completely blank.

Doris raised her hands. "Too much. This is why I was so angry when I came back. Suddenly, a bunch of the living start hounding you for answers. I need to talk to her privately." Doris seized Amelia's hand and vanished.

"No!" Darius cried.

"I hate when she does that." I straightened up. "Sorry, Darius. We won't see Amelia again until Doris has spent some time with her, and I'm not entirely sure time passes the same way for them as it does for us."

I expected him to break down, but he didn't.

"I'm going to text Brendan to pick me up. Thank you."

His calm worried me. "Are you all right?"

"No, I think I'm losing my mind." Darius shut me out and turned his attention to his phone.

"I'm really sorry if we've made everything worse."

He grimaced. "You haven't. Whether she was real or not, it was good to see Amelia again. I'll go wait on your porch, shall I?" He shrugged into his jacket and left.

"Should I go after him?" Gillian said. "Is he in shock?"

Jack said, "That's not normal."

"Nothing about this is normal. Let him be. Let's not do any more damage." I picked up Darius' bottle and took it out to the kitchen to drop in recycling. There was no way I could tell George any of this.

****

We were subdued as if all the air had been sucked out of my house. I sat at the computer and played with the ideas Darius had given me for Samantha's web site, cleaning up and ultimately sticking my work in the cloud for Mia and Ricardo to pick up and polish. Jack went out to work on the car by himself while Gillian listed some of the china and figurines that had come to me with the house for sale online.

I stretched. "Need a break, Gillian? It'll be dark soon, but we can get a walk in." I had another thought. "Instead, would you be interested in seeing if Maya and Theda are home? I'd like to pick their brains about augmented reality, and I need to do something less macabre and more normal for a bit."

"Sure. Whatever you need. We can always come back over in the evenings or next weekend. We'll be nervous about your safety until this murderer is caught. In my opinion, it's pretty clearly not Darius, regardless of what George thinks."

"Thanks. I appreciate that. But I don't want to think it's Dave, either."

Out on the road, I glanced toward the beach. I hadn't been out for my usual stroll since the murder. This was my first autumn living here. The tips of the waves sparkled like diamonds in the sun. I missed communing with the sea. There's a golden light and a warmth that has nothing to do with air temperature.

"Coming?" Gillian waited for me at the end of the walkway.

"Sorry. Daydreaming." I caught up to her, and we approached the California bungalow tucked back on the lot. "Their lawn needs works. It's scruffy."

"I sometimes forget that you've spent too much time with manicured lawns and plastic plants."

"Hey, my shrubs were live, not plastic."

Gillian laughed. "I meant that they were as good as plastic to the butterflies and other pollinators. Your neighbors have planted native grasses and flowers in their front yard. That's brome grass and oat grass and San Francisco bluegrass. There's California poppy and one of my favorites, Ithuriel's Spear. Love the purple flowers. So beautiful."

I paid more attention as we passed through an arbor and up flagstones to the wooden front door with a round porthole window set at eye level. I lifted and dropped the large, brass ring in the mouth of the lion doorknocker. "I want this door!"

"Reminds me of hobbits."

I stared at Gillian. "Somehow I can't picture you reading Tolkien."

She grinned. "I'm full of surprises."

"That you are."

The door swung inward and a voice said, "I was really tempted to swing it open and stay silent and out of sight to see what you'd do." Maya stepped out from behind the door. "But I have absolutely no patience. C'mon in." She beckoned us to follow her.

"Great house! Love the movie posters."

The hall was a gallery of metallic framed movie posters and marquees. They spanned the ages from *Indiana Jones* to Theda Bara's *Cleopatra*. We followed her through to the back porch. "Is Theda here?"

"She's over at the college helping a friend with a project. What's up?" She sat in a seagrass chair and gestured us to two more.

"You mentioned at my party that you and Theda had been film majors. Do you do anything with it now?"

Maya nodded. "That's what Theda's doing now over at Clouston. A friend of hers wrote a romance, so Theda's helping her create a book trailer."

Gillian and I exchanged a glance. "So, do you guys know anything about augmented reality?"

Chapter 11

The sun hung low in the sky as we walked back toward my place. "That was helpful. I have an idea of how it all works now."

Gillian pointed at the garage. "Light's on. My sweetie must still be working. Let's scoop him up and get something to eat."

"Works for me."

Gillian opened the door. "Ready for food?"

"More than ready. I was cleaning up. Hang on a second." He put away his tools, turned out the light, and closed and locked the door. "Pizza?"

"Not after your recent cracks about my cooking. I'm making dinner tonight. You and Gillian can chill on the couch."

Jack raised an eyebrow but wisely kept his mouth shut as we walked to the house.

"You guys wash up and relax. I'll bring you something to munch on while I cook." I headed for the kitchen and got to work.

The doorbell rang as I carried a cheese and cracker tray out to the coffee table. "I'll get it."

George stood on the threshold. "Bad time?"

"Not at all. Come on in. Let me take your jacket." I hung it on the hall tree. George followed me into the living room.

"I checked your beach before coming in," George

said with a placid face.

I froze. Doris had rescued Amelia from the beach hours ago. Had he seen something?

He laughed. "Just kidding."

Jack's laugh was a bit too hearty. "So, no more bodies?"

I glared at him and changed the subject. "The nuts are truffled Marcona almonds." I passed him the bowl.

George took the bowl and plopped his lanky frame down on the couch.

"Beer, George? I have a feeling you're going to need it," Jack said.

"Please." George set the bowl down and took a handful of almonds. "At least I can rely on Jack's friendship…until he gets his car registered." He leaned forward, elbows on knees. "We haven't let much info loose, but because there are rumors about you circulating now, I wanted to see if you were okay."

A hard lump sat in the pit of my stomach. "Thanks."

Jack handed George a bottle. "Should we be worried?"

"Cautious." George put a piece of cheese on a cracker and ate it. "Have you experienced any looky-loos or harassing phone calls?"

"Not so far, but I'm glad you're checking. Gillian and I will leave soon."

"Couldn't you have been more reassuring?" I snarled.

"Not if you want truth." George took a handful of nuts. "If you're recording tonight's news, you'll see we released a statement that says you had no part in this murder despite the proximity to your house. Several of the inquiries and comments made to the department were getting nasty. I hope that takes some pressure off you. As I said, there've been quite a few rumors."

"Ricardo and Mia mentioned it. I hope it doesn't affect our business. I've been waiting for the villagers with torches and pitchforks." I finished my wine. "Is everyone ready for dinner? George, you staying? There's plenty."

"In that case." He carried his beer to the table.

The meal was simple: salmon, new potatoes, peas, and a salad. But I cooked it and made my point. Jack could have his beloved pizza tomorrow.

"How are you enjoying living in Las Lunas?" Jack asked George. "Do you miss Hawaii?"

"I often do. There's no place else on Earth quite like them."

"Them?" Gillian asked.

"The isles, the haunted isles." George looked into the distance.

Gillian speared a piece of salmon. "I thought the British Isles were the Haunted Isles. Elves and pixies."

"Menehune." George smiled. "I guess both are haunted by the Old Ones. Hmm. I wonder if that's true of all islands. Iceland has the Hidden People, the Huldufólk."

"The hidden people?" she asked.

"Iceland is the Garden where Adam and Eve lived…if you're an Icelander. Once God came to visit them, but Eve, who was washing her children at the time, only got half their large number washed, so she hid the rest to prevent God from seeing the dirty ones. God knew, of course, and said that those who had been hidden from him would also remain hidden from humans."

"I didn't know you were interested in folklore." I passed him the peas.

"I like islands. All islands. I suspect it's because you don't have to go far to get to the water, which is also why I'm living at the coast. I spent a week in Iceland once looking for northern lights, soaking in the Blue Lagoon, and taking a Super Jeep tour that included glaciers and geysers. My guide told me about the Hidden People and even said that building projects were rerouted to avoid annoying them. Islanders have respect for those they share their habitats with…unlike many mainlanders."

I narrowed my eyes at him. "Are you pulling my leg?"

"Not at all. You've always called me superstitious, but maybe I merely know a bit more about the hidden world than you do." He smiled and ate a bite of potato.

As he said this, Doris shimmered in the corner behind him.

I bit my tongue. "Perhaps I misjudged you."

Jack and Gillian shared a look, and I almost told him there and then but hesitated a moment too long. "Are you ready for coffee and dessert?"

"Sounds good," he said.

"I'll help you." Gillian put her napkin next to her plate and followed me into the kitchen where she turned to me. "Are you going to tell him about Doris tonight?"

I blew out a breath. "I seriously considered it, but things are going so well. I don't want to jinx it." I shook my head. "Much as I want to, I think our relationship is too fragile."

"Don't wait too long." Gillian carried the tray of

tartlets to the table.

I followed with the coffee.

George glanced at his phone. "I have to go." He stood, took a sip of coffee, and grabbed a tartlet. "I'm sure I'll be seeing you all again soon."

"Wait!" I said. "Is it about the murder?"

George nodded but went out the front door without saying anything more, his phone up to his ear.

"He really is the most frustrating man! Good thing I didn't go out to dinner with him. It would have been a short date."

After George left, Doris joined us in the kitchen as we cleaned up. "When are you going to tell him about me?"

"I saw you shimmering in the corner. Thanks for not scaring him, Doris. How's Amelia?"

She shook her head. "As I told you, I have no idea how I got here or how to leave. People talk about 'summoning' ghosts. No one asked me if I wanted to show up, and I doubt if anyone asked her."

"Do you regret being here?"

She paused. "I don't, but she might. Being back here has brought back some of my memories. Being in my mother's house again, seeing her needlework, the rooms where I played as a child, even the beach where I died." Her clothes shifted to a black mourning dress complete with veil. "I think Amelia is reliving a trauma she doesn't understand in a place that's unfamiliar to her."

"Where is she?"

Doris pointed at the couch where Amelia had lain earlier. "She's working on control."

"Is there anything we can do to help her?"

"Just don't scream while she's working on this. You living can be pretty scary at times."

I turned toward Gillian and Jack, who stared at the couch. "Got that?"

Gillian nodded, but Jack said, "I can't believe we have two of them!"

Doris made a moue. "It's hard being a ghost. I can inhabit Thor, but I can't pet him. I miss soft cat fur. I miss warm fires. I miss butterfly wings."

"I'm sorry, Doris. But at least you still have some senses like hearing and seeing without a corporeal body even if you can't touch or feel sensations."

"But I can't smell your bouquet of pretty flowers on the mantel."

I looked over at the vase and noticed that a Stargazer lily had shed some of its petals. I went over and picked them up. "These are poisonous to Thor." I threw them into my new red kitchen trashcan. "He won't be able to get at them in there."

"You really are only half there," Jack said.

And Doris vanished.

"Jack!" I yelled and clapped my hand over my mouth, remembering Doris' words of warning. I turned to reassure Amelia, but she was gone, too. "Rats."

He held up his hands. "I wasn't trying to upset her. I was curious."

"Try to restrain your curiosity." I glowered.

"Something else I was curious about. George doesn't know about Doris. George knows you have a cat. How about Doris possesses Thor and walks with me on a leash straight into the police station? I'm still working with George on getting my car registered as an historic vehicle. I can ask for some water for Thoris, take her off the leash, and reengage George's attention. Thoris can wander around the police station and gather some intel for us. What do you think?"

Doris' head reappeared. "I think that's hunky dory."

Chapter 12

The next morning we put our plan into effect. As soon as Jack and Thoris left for their meeting with George at the station, Gillian and I went to find Dave and Niles. I'd seen a lot more of George in the past few days than I had of Dave, and that was not normal. I wondered what was going on with those two.

I knocked at Dave's patio door and saw movement inside, but he didn't answer. "Dave, it's me, Cass. Gillian's with me. We need to talk to you."

The door opened. The room was dark. He hadn't turned on any lights, and the blinds were drawn. I stepped in despite the gloom, and Gillian followed me. Dave stood behind the door and shut it as we entered.

"Can we turn a light on?" I asked.

He flipped the switch next to the door, and the lava lamp burped sluggishly orange in the corner. Ragged didn't even begin to describe the condition he was in. He hadn't shaved or combed his hair. He wore only pajama bottoms. His feet were bare. But the most disturbing thing was that Dave, the consummate host, didn't greet us or offer us anything to drink. I'd never entered his house before without those amenities.

"Dave, where's Niles?"

He shook himself and smiled wanly. "Hi, Cass. Gillian. Welcome to my humble—and somewhat messy—abode. Niles might still be at the police station or he could be at the hospital by now. I don't know."

"Is he okay?" I asked.

Gillian said, "Do they suspect him?"

"I don't know if they suspect him. I know they suspect me. They asked him if he'd go with them to answer some questions. I've been up, thinking about everything that's happened. It all hit me. I'll never see Aunt Amelia again. I didn't think I'd miss her this much. It's like losing my mom all over again. There didn't seem to be any reason to get dressed today."

"Dave, there has to be a party somewhere." I tried to appeal to his sense of fun. He snorted, and I realized I'd never heard Dave express any cynicism before. Regret, yes. Cynicism, no. "What happened? Something else must have happened."

He ran his fingers through his tousled hair. "Maybe the cops think I did it." Tears welled in his eyes.

"But you didn't do it. Want to come over to my place for some lunch?"

His front door on the street side opened, and Niles walked in followed by George's partner Bill and a uniformed officer.

"This is a search warrant." All business, Detective Daniels handed a folded paper to Dave, who took it, hand shaking.

"What are you looking for?" I asked.

Bill looked me up and down. "Do you live here?"

"You know I don't."

"Then I suggest you leave. Now."

"Go, Cass. It'll be okay." Dave opened his patio door for us, and Gillian and I left.

"How rude!" I had a mind to stay and argue, but Gillian pulled me away.

"We'll find out what's going on from Dave after they leave, and maybe Jack will come back with some information. They're only doing their job."

I still fumed. "It's obvious Dave is mourning Amelia. He clearly wouldn't hurt her."

"The cops are just following the evidence. We all like Dave, but how much do you really know about him? Niles seems like the stalwart one. Funny that he didn't say anything to us."

"The police interrogation probably scared him, too. That settles it. They're obviously getting it wrong. We have to figure out who murdered Amelia."

We reached my house, and Gillian opened the back door for me. "Jack and I are leaving in a couple of days. There's not much we can do in that time, and if you stir up a hornet's nest, we won't be here to help you. Who else is there?"

"Ricardo and Mia."

"Students who attend class."

"Mina."

"We haven't seen her since before Halloween."

I rubbed my chin. "That alone is strange. I hope she's okay. We should go by to check on her."

"Good idea, but first let's have lunch in front of the TV and see what info they've released to the public."

"We can fill in the spreadsheet Jack started."

We slapped together some sandwiches and parked in the living room in front of the TV. Gillian took control of the remote, and I opened the laptop. We didn't have much on the spreadsheet. The headings were Suspect, Means, Motive, Opportunity, and Scene of Crime. Jack had already entered Dave, Niles, Darius, Gerry, and Unknown.

"Gillian?"

She located the show she wanted and stopped before hitting Play. "Huh?"

"What about Gerry?"

"The accountant? Don't know. I really didn't pay him much attention. He sort of blended into the woodwork at Amelia's dinner. Didn't George tell us he was missing?"

"He said running didn't make him look innocent, but he didn't say anything about evidence against him."

"You don't suppose the cops have him locked up, do you?"

"Wouldn't the reporters have mentioned that?"

She twisted to look at the TV. "I didn't see anything about him."

"How would you know? You're on pause." At her outraged expression, I laughed. "I'm teasing. George wouldn't have told us he was missing if they had him locked up. But I think we should catch up on what the police have been releasing to the public."

Gillian scanned through the recorded news shows.

I leaned back. "Not a mention of Gerry Waverley. I wonder if the reporters are even aware of him."

Gillian paused the recording. "If the police consider him a suspect or a person of interest, you'd think they'd have given out that information. Media, particularly social media, can be a powerful tool to locate people."

"True." Now the hard columns to fill in. Means. I heard the front door open and close and called out, "Jack? You back?"

Thor came running in and sat at my feet.

I looked down. "Tuna juice?"

Thor meowed.

"Coming right up." I went into the kitchen and set a brimming saucer on the floor. I'd set it aside when I drained the can of fish for tuna salad.

Jack walked over to the table, took a look at the computer screen, and sat down. "Been busy while we've been gone."

"How'd the visit with George go?" Gillian asked.

"I'll be able to take you all for a ride in the convertible very soon. Doris will have to tell you what she found out. Lunch? We're both hungry, not just Thor."

"Okay. Gillian and I have already eaten." I set out lunch choices as Jack and Gillian came in and sat down at the trestle table.

"Doris, want to join us?" I asked.

Doris faded in sitting on the counter as usual. She could barely contain herself with glee. "That was peachy keen!"

"Peachy keen?" I opened a bag of chips and poured some in a bowl for Jack.

"Real cool?" She tilted her head coquettishly.

Gillian passed the ham to Jack. "What did you find out?"

"I wish I could draw or use a camera," Doris said. "But I'd be happy to go back and have another look. The officers all loved me particularly when I rubbed against them and purred, which meant I could get up on desks to read papers."

"Did you see the letters DNA?" Jack opened a beer.

"All over the place. It was on those little yellow papers on a board. It was the heading on several things.

Darius, Niles, and Dave were tested. Inconclusive. Money was the big motive for Niles and Dave, but jealousy and revenge for Darius. There was a note that Amelia complained about him bothering her."

I looked at Gillian. "Restraining order?"

"They had a sheet like yours." Doris nodded toward Jack. "Means. Motive. Opportunity. Their aunt controlled the grandmother's trust, which was earmarked to support Dave. He got the house and the income. Niles didn't like that. They wrote student loans next to his name."

"Who else was on the spreadsheet?" I took another bite.

"You were."

"Seriously? Motive?"

"One of the detectives thought you might be a clever serial killer. They talked about you and teased George."

"Oh, great! There goes any hope for…" They all looked at me. "Never mind. Who else?"

"Jack and Gillian because there are murders whenever they visit."

It was Jack's turn to get indignant. "That's lame!"

Gillian poured me another glass of lemonade.

I snickered. "Who else?"

"Gerry Waverley. They had an entry for a random, unrelated serial killer. They had a list of suspicious people they'd arrested or observed in the area. They had pictures of people, including all of you, out on the beach."

"Great." I brought out the chocolate chip shortbread.

"What about opportunity?" Gillian asked.

"Everyone had opportunity, but they don't know where she was killed. George told Bill that until they find out, alibis are squishy."

Jack laughed. "Technical term."

"Did you hear any other conversations that were interesting?"

"They told George your house is haunted. They told him everyone knows you have a ghost. They know he's superstitious, and they tease him. They joked that he might be in love with a serial killer. His partner makes them stop. He thought he was fitting in pretty well until the second murder on your beach. Now he wonders if he will ever fit in here. He thinks maybe he should leave."

"Stop. I don't want to hear any more." My sandwich sat like a fist in my stomach.

Doris wavered. "Cass, you should tell him about me."

"No!" I yelled, a bit too loud.

Doris vanished.

That was the second time I'd yelled after she asked me not to. "Doris, I didn't mean it." But there wasn't even a whisper of her.

Jack said, "I'm going to enter all this into the spreadsheet. If we're implicated at all even in jest, we need to pay closer attention to what's going on."

"Don't worry. If you leave, Cass, Doris will come back. Jack, why don't you get the details from Doris? Cass, you said you were worried about Mina, why don't we go look for her?"

I sighed and got up. "I didn't mean to hurt Doris' feelings."

"I know, and she does, too. You know, that wasn't

a bad idea. If you tell him the whole truth and introduce him to Doris, you wouldn't have to cover things up and make excuses."

"But I could lose him."

"Maybe, but do you have him now? Meeting Doris was a bit of an adjustment for all of us, but your relationship isn't going to progress unless you're honest with him."

I changed the subject. "Let's go find Mina and ask her why she hasn't been around. Maybe she saw or heard something that would help solve this murder or at the very least clear Dave. I'm worried about him."

The weather was wild today. Wind whipped up the surf and white caps hurtled into the rocks. I wrapped a scarf around my head and neck even though Mina's house was only up the hill. As we approached, a light in the parlor window beckoned, and the curtain moved slightly. She was there. I exhaled and relaxed. I hoped she would answer the door.

We climbed the steps, but the door didn't open so I knocked.

At the third rap, she opened the door a crack. "Yes?"

"Hi, Mina, Gillian and I would like to talk to you." She closed the door, and I thought she was indicating that we should leave. But the chain rattled, and she let us in. She latched and locked the door behind us. I'd never known her to lock her door, but then again I hadn't lived here long.

"Tea? I have gunpowder today," she asked as she led us into the parlor.

"Lemon bars?" I asked.

"Of course," she said, smiling as she seated herself

on the edge of a gold brocade upholstered Queen Anne chair. She poured the steaming liquid into two delicate porcelain cups, handed them to us, and then proffered napkins, small plates with a lily of the valley design, and a tray of lemon bars…like magic.

"You'll love these, Gillian," I said, taking one. I waited for her reaction after her first bite.

Her eyes widened and she nodded. "These are amazing! Tart with just a touch of sweet. So lemony!"

They were as delicious as they had been the first time. After a sip of the strong tea, I turned to Mina.

"That's the first time I've ever seen you lock a door much less put the chain on."

Mina pursed her lips. "Things are a bit different here right now."

I set my cup down. "Do you blame me?"

"Of course not, dear. You are not to blame."

"I'm happy to hear you say that. It's an opinion not shared by many of your neighbors…or the police."

"They're your neighbors, too, and those who are important believe in you." She refreshed my cup.

"I'm glad to hear it because I really like it here. I feel at home. I didn't think I would. I was very fond of my life in Pleasanton, but finding out that my friends there were all fair weather ones was quite the shock. And then there's something about this place. It's cozy, and the sea sings me to sleep at night."

Mina smiled and offered me another lemon bar. Then she grew serious. "I'm glad you like it here, but you must be careful. There is a murderer here. One that I feel is very dangerous, very ruthless. Nothing will stand between this murderer and the prize."

"The prize?" Gillian asked.

"The motivation for all this drama. It's a dangerous time, and it's very close to us. Please latch all your windows and lock your doors. I fear the killer isn't through yet."

"Do you have any idea who it might be?" I asked.

"It isn't someone who belongs here."

At first I felt relief that it couldn't be Dave or Darius because they live here. My relief dissipated quickly as I thought about her exact words. She hadn't said "someone from here." She'd said it wasn't someone who "belongs" here. I wondered if she meant a stranger or a resident who shouldn't be here. Both Darius and Dave were transplants like me. I hadn't noticed anyone unusual, but then again I didn't yet know everyone in town.

"The police aren't telling us much," Gillian said.

Mina leaned back and smiled. "The joy of a small-town constabulary is that they live in and know the community. They pay attention. They attend the AARP chapter meetings to tell us about scams. They get to know the kids at the high school and take the Boy Scouts on tours of the jail."

"That's lovely," Gillian said. "But what's AARP?"

Mina's laugh was high and flute-like. "You're still young. It's the association for us old folk. I don't remember what the acronym stands for now, but it was something about retired people. A lot of people I know who belong aren't retired."

"The responsiveness of the local police does make me feel safer," I conceded. "I wish George would be more open with me."

Mina cocked her head, reminding me of an inquisitive heron. "Are you being open with him?"

I opened my mouth, but I knew I wasn't.

"You want to mean more to him than his job. I know. A lot of women have felt that way over the ages." She refreshed my cup again. "It's hard to trust people these days."

George had asked me to trust him. Did I not trust him? I wasn't sure. Maybe I just didn't like feeling left out. "I have a stake in this. People think I had something to do with this."

"Some people," Gillian added.

"You know the door under my porch?" Mina asked.

"I noticed that," I said. "I was curious about it. Your front door is quite high up. Is there a floor under this one?"

"It's not a full floor. It's more like an unfinished basement. My father built this house many years ago, and he used the space as a workshop for his furniture making and reupholstering. That door doesn't lock. If you ever need a place to hide quickly, go there. You'll be safe."

I had visions of cobwebs, spiders, and mice. "Thanks, Mina."

Mina lifted the top to the pot and peered in. "Will you be wanting more tea?"

I set my cup and saucer down on the tray. "No, thanks. We need to be going." I stood.

Gillian set her plate down and stood, also. "Thanks so much for tea and for the offer of refuge."

"You're welcome."

Mina showed us out. The lock clicked behind us. Gillian and I exchanged a look, and a chill shot up my spine as we walked back to the bungalow.

"I've never seen her so spooked. The last time I saw her this nervous was when I first moved in. She visited me and kept looking around for ghosts."

As we reached my door and entered, I thought perhaps I should start locking my own door as Jack requested, at least until the murderer was arrested.

"About time you guys got back."

"What's up, Jack?" I hung my jacket on the hall tree.

"Please call Samantha. She's called about a half dozen times. Seems she and Darius have been talking." He looked at me meaningfully.

"Uh oh."

"Exactly."

Chapter 13

"How're we going to handle this?"

Gillian hung her jacket up. "We can't. We have no way to contact Amelia, and even if we did, Samantha can be pretty overwhelming. We can't turn her loose on the poor woman. Ghost."

Jack smirked. "You do realize you're trying to protect a ghost. Hello. She's already dead. Not much else can happen to her."

Gillian shot him a dirty look.

I ignored him. "I do have to call Samantha back. She may contact me at any moment. I'd rather not be blindsided. Any ideas?"

"Nope." Jack didn't look up from the computer but continued to work on the spreadsheet.

"Don't think he wants to talk to her again," I whispered to Gillian.

Gillian nodded and gestured toward the kitchen. "Let's do some brainstorming."

I followed her. "Figure out something?"

"I need coffee. Sit."

I sat and waited. When she put a mug in front of me and sat down with hers, I said, "Ideas?"

She sipped. "We need Doris' help but maybe one or two thoughts." She took another sip and set the mug down. "Okay, this could get out of hand really quickly. I know you don't want to, but you should call her immediately, invite her over, and be straight with her. We need to enlist Doris and let her know what she's going to be in for. Samantha will not be happy to hear that Doris has never seen her fiancé on the beach."

"Or she might be happy because it means he moved on."

Gillian shook her head. "That's optimistic. It doesn't give her closure. That's the downside of believing in ghosts or even knowing that they exist. Knowing that, you want to talk to your own loved ones."

I nodded. "I get it. If it's possible, you ask why not me? Why do other people get to talk to their loved ones?"

Gillian took another sip. "And she may not be happy that we haven't told her about Doris before this."

"True. Go warn Jack. I'll call her."

"Will do."

I took a deep breath and tapped on Samantha's number in my contacts list. "Hey, Samantha."

"Hi, Cass. I planned to come over to visit today." Her voice sounded tight.

"Oh, good. I was calling to invite you over."

She didn't answer right away, and when she did, I heard the surprise in her voice. "Really?"

"Yes, I want to tell you something I think you'll be very interested in." I held my breath.

"Good. What time should I come?"

"We'll be home the rest of the day. Come any time you like."

"I'll see you soon." She hung up.

I put my phone on the charger, picked up my coffee cup, and joined them at the dining room table.

"She's coming soon. Want to hide?"

Jack looked like he was thinking about it. "No. I assume you're going to introduce her to Doris."

"If Doris responds. I clearly don't understand the afterlife."

He snorted.

****

An hour later, Samantha swept in. As usual, she'd dressed dramatically. She reminded me of a zaftig redheaded zebra. It was an illusion brought on by the vertical black and white stripes of her wide legged pantsuit. Her earrings were huge rings of mother-of-pearl half hidden in her long, wavy red hair.

"C'mon in, Samantha. Want me to take your jacket?"

"No, I'll unbutton it." She did, revealing a fitted black silk blouse. She did a quick scan of the room. "I've heard some interesting things from Darius."

I was so tempted to say 'Really? What have you heard?' but I wasn't in the mood for games. "He told you about Doris and Amelia."

Meeting no resistance, she nodded and relaxed a notch. "He did."

"Have a seat." She and I joined Jack and Gillian at the table. "We haven't heard from Amelia since then."

Samantha's eyes narrowed, on guard again.

"She's telling the truth." Gillian leaned forward on her elbows. "We'll try to get them to show, but we wanted to forewarn you. We don't have any control over them."

Samantha arched her left eyebrow.

"Seriously." I glanced up toward the ceiling. "Doris, are you there? We want to introduce you to

Samantha."

Nothing.

I closed my eyes to avoid Samantha's glare and whispered, "Pretty please, Doris? We need you."

"About time you admitted it."

At first her voice was disembodied. I heaved a sigh of relief as she materialized very slowly from glimmer to transparent.

"Doris, this is our friend Samantha. Samantha, this is Doris, my resident ghost."

Doris, still transparent, curtsied. I wondered if something was wrong. This was an opportunity for her to ham it up. Normally, she would have taken full advantage.

Samantha did what most of us do and poked Doris. Doris' form lost definition. Gillian and I exchanged glances. Even Jack paid attention now. Something was wrong.

"Is Amelia with you? Can you call her? Do you see others on the beach? Are there other ghosts in this house?" Samantha scoured the corners as if ghosts hid in the corners of the room.

"No. I'm alone. I'm sorry." And Doris was gone.

"Where'd she go? I have more questions."

I put a hand on Samantha's forearm. "I know. None of us understands what's going on with Amelia. We haven't seen her since that initial appearance."

Samantha opened her mouth, but Gillian cut in. "Doris didn't look right tonight."

"What do you mean?" Samantha frowned.

Gillian gesticulated. "Ordinarily, she's, I don't know, perky. That's a dreadful word. She's usually full of life. Uh, she's usually energetic...for someone who's dead." She looked at me for help, her eyebrows peaked.

"I think Gillian's trying to say that Doris generally appears more vibrant. It's as if she's been drained of energy. It might have something to do with Amelia." I shook my head. "But I have no idea how."

"How long have you been talking to Doris?"

The question I'd been dreading. There was no getting around it. "Almost from the beginning."

She nodded and rolled her lips inward. "So all the time I was out filming on your beach…"

I hate innuendo. "Yeah, pretty much."

I guess I deserved all this for not being honest with her in the first place. I'd thought she was amusing out there in her weird outfits with her camera trying to film ghosts. I hadn't taken her seriously. What goes around comes around.

I took a deep breath and exhaled. "I apologize. I was not honest with you." George's face flashed though my mind. Guiltily, I banished the image. "I'll…we'll answer any questions you have now."

"How many ghosts have you seen?"

"Just the two."

"No men?"

"No. Only Doris and Amelia."

She considered this. "Would you be willing to have a séance to see if we can reach a specific person who's passed on?"

"I don't want you to be disappointed."

The glare she gave me could have fried eggs to a blackened crisp.

"Okay. Sure. Whatever I can do to help." I ignored the warning look Jack shot me.

Samantha stood, chin in the air. "I'll get back to

you with the details."

"Anytime." I contritely followed her to the door to show her out.

When she left, I leaned against the jamb. "Hoo boy."

"At least she didn't fire you from the web site job." Gillian managed a weak smile.

"Not yet," Jack added.

"What are we going to do?"

"Hold a séance." Jack snapped the laptop shut.

Gillian got up. "I'm making you another cup of coffee."

"Thanks." I sat back down at the table. "Jack, what do you think about Doris' condition?"

My cell rang. "Ricardo." I swiped. "Hey, Ricardo. Mind if I put you on speaker? I want to drink my coffee while it's still hot."

"No problem. Why are you drinking coffee at this hour?"

"Nerves. Samantha came by to see the ghosts."

"Did she?"

"She met Doris, who seems to be out of sorts."

Gillian set a fresh mug of coffee in front of me. She gestured at Jack, who nodded. She returned to the kitchen.

"Is she all right?"

"I don't think either Doris or Samantha is all right. We're close to releasing the web site for Crystalline, but I worried that, by not telling her about Doris in the first place, I blew our contract. I'm sorry, Ricardo."

"One thing I've learned working for her, Samantha's bark is often much scarier than her nip. She's really a softy. She wouldn't cancel on me."

"She wants a séance."

"A real séance?"

"Yup."

"Wow. Okay. Did you agree?"

"I was in no position to refuse her anything."

"No problem. We can do it."

Jack chimed in. "You realize that she wants a real *real* séance."

"You guys are stressing, aren't you?" Ricardo asked.

"How could you tell?"

"Cass, two of your neighbors used to do séances at your house. Chill. With all of us and Dave and Mina, it won't be a problem. They'll know what to do. C'mon. It'll be fun. Oh and by the way, Bobbo's interested in us doing a web site for his comic shop. Hasta." He hung up.

"I guess he called to tell us about the new job." My phone chimed the disconnect.

Gillian said, "At least he's not worried."

Jack stretched. "We'll sort it out in the morning. Try not to worry, sis."

"C'mon, lover boy." Gillian tugged on his sleeve. They took their coffee and retired.

"Night, kids. I'll lock up."

I flipped on the security lights and looked out the back door. All was peaceful and quiet. Even the waves had calmed down, merely lapping the shore. Thinking of Mina, I put the chain on, added my mug to the dishwasher, and ran it. Back in the living room, I turned on the light in my loft, took one last look around, and ascended the stairs to bed.

Chapter 14

Friday morning I woke up and stretched. I had the sense of others sharing the bungalow with me. I felt warm and cozy and safe. No point in wasting time, though. I got up, dressed, and headed downstairs to start breakfast. On the spiral staircase, I heard voices and hurried to the bottom to find my neighbors seated at the trestle table.

"Dave! Niles! You two are up early." I was so happy to see Dave up, shaved, and dressed. Niles, on the other hand, looked a little ragged.

"I got off shift a half hour ago." Niles raised one shoulder and then the other, rolling them and working out the kinks.

Gillian, wearing my long, white apron to protect her lavender sweater, turned around with a spatula in her hand. "Eggs?"

"Where's Jack?"

"Taking an early morning stroll to check the car."

"Of course. What was I thinking?" I tied the red gingham apron on and moved to help.

"We should be able to take you for a ride before we leave Sunday."

"You're leaving?" Niles looked up.

"No choice. Our jobs are over in the East Bay where we live. Duty calls."

"I guess I thought you lived somewhere close by."

Gillian sighed. "As I explained to Cass, it is close. Rush hour traffic gets in the way is all."

He furrowed his brow and stroked the side of his jaw.

"Don't worry. We'll keep an eye on Cass," Dave said.

On closer inspection, his eyes were rimmed with dark circles, and there was no spark of joy in them.

"Sure thing." Niles was a beat behind Dave.

"I'll have to finish feeding you then." Gillian turned back to the stove.

When the last of the food was on the table, Gillian and I joined them.

"So, Dave, what was the search warrant for?" I picked up my fork, slid some eggs onto my plate, and looked at Dave, who glanced sideways at Niles.

Niles wiped his mouth. "After they showed him the warrant, they put him out in the car. I followed them around as much as they'd let me. They took every knife in the house and Dave's spear gun."

I remembered Amelia's cut throat.

The bacon was nearly gone by the time Jack got back. "Glad you saved me some." Jack squirted lemon detergent on his hands and turned on the water to rinse.

"There is hand soap, Jack." I eyed the soapy splashes on the counter and raised an eyebrow.

"Yes'm." He sheepishly wiped up with a dishcloth. Then he grabbed a crispy bacon slice from the platter and plopped down beside Gillian. "Dave. Nice to see you again, Niles."

Niles took a sip of coffee. "The hospital let me have off a few days because of Aunt Amelia's death." He was talkative, telling us about the hospital and the staff and their quirks. He had us laughing by the time we finished eating.

Dave leaned back and patted his stomach. "Thanks for breakfast. I should get back to try to find the rest of the trust stuff."

"Heard anything about the accountant?" I asked.

Dave shrugged a shoulder. "No. We have an appointment with the lawyer, though." He turned toward the door. "Sorry. We've got to go."

I smiled. "Always nice to see you."

He nodded and slipped out the door.

"He seems worried," Gillian said.

Niles watched him go. "Don't worry. I'll take care of him." He smiled and followed Dave out.

"I'm worried about Dave," I said. "And I'm thinking George is right and the accountant did it. What innocent person vanishes like that?"

"Niles is charming." Gillian cleared the table. "At least they're talking to the lawyer. That's a good sign."

"This is the last business day before the weekend, and we're leaving on Sunday, so I want to finish up any paperwork I have to sign for the car. However, we can put in some more time on the spreadsheet. See if we can figure anything out. Personally, I'd rather it were Niles or Darius than Dave." Jack looked at his watch. "And we should plan that séance, don't you think?"

"Uh huh." I nodded absentmindedly as I got up and looked out my back window to watch Dave and Niles walk across the beach. Something was bugging me, but it wouldn't come into focus. I turned away. "Guess I'd better do some research on séances." I moved to the dining room table, opened my laptop, and stared at the screen.

Doris appeared. "I can help there."

"Good to see you…solid…I mean, thicker—"

She held up a hand, stopping my ramble. "Got it, Toots. I'm getting better. Amelia's an energy drain. Not sure why." She shook herself although, in her case, it was more of a shimmy. "So, I hear we're doing a séance." She rubbed her hands together. "Hotcha!"

"Glad you're on board with this. I'm going to need help." I entered a few search terms.

Doris passed her hand through the screen and shivered.

I looked up. "You okay?"

She nodded but cocked her head to one side. "When I pass through these things, we don't meet. They don't know I'm here, but I feel them."

"You don't 'meet'?"

"When I pass through you, we meet." She smiled. "I feel you. I feel you respond to me when I pass through you. I know you don't like it, but I do. It's deeper."

"But you feel the energy in computers and cell phones?"

"Sort of. It's not the same. They aren't alive even though they have energy."

I began to understand. "Could you interact with them? Change data?"

She looked puzzled.

"Look." I pointed to my laptop screen again and tapped a few keys, bringing my laptop back to life. Then I opened a blank document and typed: Doris is my friend.

Doris read it and smiled.

"Now, can you change the words or the spelling?"

143

She moved into the keyboard and vanished. My computer went all wonky, and I had a moment of panic. Then the words changed on the screen: Cass is my friend. Doris stepped out, and her tiny figure paused on the frame of the keyboard and looked back at her handiwork.

"Is this what you meant?" Her voice was as tiny as her figure.

"Perfect. Was it hard to do?"

"I had to figure out where the spirit of the words lived."

I opened my mouth and shut it again. Did she mean where the code was? I suspected we were having a semantic disconnect. "Do you think you could do the same thing on other devices like a text message on a phone?" I pulled out my phone and typed a message to my brother: *Hi, Jack.* I put the phone on the table.

Doris floated to the table, stepped onto the phone, and vanished.

This was magic, and the little child in me responded. Then my adult self put the brakes on my superstitious mind: no, this was merely undiscovered science. Sometimes I was such a party pooper.

The message changed to "*hijack.*" Doris emerged from the phone, triggering the send function.

Jack's phone pinged. He shook his head and typed.

"Did you do that on purpose?" I asked Doris.

"What?"

"Did you intentionally send the message?"

Doris looked down at the phone. "No."

"We'll have to work on your technique."

My phone pinged. A message from Jack: *Really? I thought you gave up on that joke long ago.*

I texted back: *That was from Doris.*

Jack: *Say hi.*

"He says hi."

"I can see that."

The phone in my hand rang, and I jumped. "Hello?"

"Hi, Cass. It's Ricardo. Mia and I wanted to get back to you about the séance."

"When do you want to get together?"

"Can we swing by at noon? We'll bring lunch. Mia's mom—I'm still getting used to calling her that—made a mess of spaghetti and garlic bread yesterday, and you know it's much better the second day."

"I do. That sounds great. Come by any time. I'm not going anywhere."

"Will do." He hung up.

"When are they coming?" Gillian asked.

"Any time. They're bringing lunch."

"Y'know, I can really get into your friends providing you with food," Jack said. "Last visit we nearly starved."

"Don't give her a hard time, Jack, or you'll find yourself starving when we get home."

"I'm delighted because my restaurant bill is much lower on this trip." I made a moue at Jack.

"Touché. I'm going out to the car and calling George to get that ball rolling. I'll be back to help. Gillian?"

Gillian pointed at Jack and then herself, smiled, and followed him out.

"Doris, let's not tell anyone else about your ability for now."

"Fine with me."

"I'd better take another look at Samantha's web site before they get here."

I played with her web site for a while, but my desire to solve the murder got the better of me, and I returned to the spreadsheet. Jack had entered all the information he and Thoris had gotten from their visit to the police station. I thought about motive. The police might suspect me, Jack, and Gillian, but I knew better and didn't waste time.

Instead, I went to the Motive column. I'd thought Darius didn't have a motive because of his great love for Amelia, but love could be jealous and demanding. What if he had the idea that, if he couldn't have her, no one could? Jack had typed jealousy and revenge in the column. I added abuse. For Dave we had money, and the same for Niles. I leaned back in the chair. The accountant. Why wasn't the accountant getting back to Niles and Dave? Where was he and what motive did he have for killing his employer? Or was he also dead? I needed to ask George.

Opportunity. Darius' alibi was shaky. I had no idea who had an alibi, but at that hour of the night, most people probably wouldn't. That was my next quest.

It was early, but I thought I heard Ricardo and Mia and went to open the door. There was no one there. I stepped out onto the porch and looked around. The beach was deserted, but Mina was rocking on her balcony. I must have been mistaken.

I wasn't particularly worried. I'd gotten used to the creaks and groans of my old Arts and Crafts bungalow. At first, they freaked me out, but with Doris popping out of nowhere and Dave's frequent rat-a-tats on my back door, not much concerned me now.

I'd heard all the stories about local ghosts and strange sights on the beach, but once I'd met the real thing, mere stories didn't scare me.

Chapter 15

Half an hour later I heard chatter and laughter out front. Ricardo and Mia arrived, followed by Jack and Gillian. The minute they entered, the aroma of garlicky, tomatoey spaghetti sauce hit me with its delicious, tangy richness.

"I'm hungry just smelling it." My mouth watered as I followed them into the kitchen.

Mia laughed, and it made me feel good that her life had gotten so much better. "It is delicious. Mom still misses Dad, but she's enjoying cooking for me now that I'm living with her. Her idea of portion size is a bit skewed, though."

Ricardo carried a bag into the kitchen. "My mother's the same. She's old school. Food is love."

I'd set the table while waiting for them, so we only had to heat up the food and add blood orange olive oil and white balsamic vinegar dressing to the salad.

"I checked out the latest iteration of Samantha's web site. I like that you've deemphasized her videos and emphasized her jewelry. That'll draw more business to her site. Is she okay with that?"

Ricardo nodded. "Oh, yeah. She's discovered other sites where she can display some of her ghost photography. She's dragging Brendan kicking and screaming into the twenty-first century now that they will both have web sites through us." He laughed.

"Finding these other spirit photographers has given Samantha new purpose and a lot less loneliness." Mia abruptly raised her hand to her mouth.

"What's wrong?" I asked.

"Loneliness. I thought about Professor Stone." She swallowed hard.

"How's he doing?" Gillian stuck serving spoons in the spaghetti and carried it to the table.

"He's still a suspect, but at least they haven't arrested him." Ricardo set the garlic bread on the table.

"We're worried about Dave and Niles. The police had a warrant to search Dave's place." I stirred the iced tea.

Jack hefted a couple of beers and the pitcher of iced tea. "Gillian and I have to leave in a couple of days. Is there anything we can do to help?"

Ricardo shook his head. "Not really. We're trying to be sympathetic, and I'm still putting in hours at Crystalline for Samantha as well as creating her web site."

"I'm trying to get him to quit working for Bobbo," Mia added. "It's too much."

Ricardo sat next to her. "Not yet. When he signs a contract for a web site…maybe."

"Okay then," I said. "This is your deal, Ricardo. Do you want to do the presentation for Samantha?"

"Yes, and I want her to feel as though she's a special client." He helped himself to the spaghetti and passed the bowl to Gillian who sat down at the end of the table.

"I'm good with that. Now, I'm assuming that her séance will be here in my loft."

"That's what we were thinking." Mia smiled.

"We need to decide first what kind of séance this will be: real or staged," I said.

"I think it has to be real," Mia said. "Otherwise, we're not playing fair."

"Besides," Ricardo said, "don't you want to know what might be out there? Pass the garlic bread."

"I already know that ghosts exist." I gestured toward Doris, who was sitting on the back of the couch, watching us. "If we fake it, Samantha will experience something; if we don't, we have no idea if anyone or anything will appear. I'm also a little leery of calling something weird up."

Mia buttered a piece of bread. "Have you ever asked Mina if anything strange occurred during a séance here?"

"From what she's told me, I think Doris' appearance was the strangest thing they experienced."

"The story goes that they wanted to conjure up a permanent resident ghost as a muse for their writing group," Ricardo said. "We won't be trying for a roommate for Doris. We only want to contact Samantha's fiancé and ask his permission for her to be involved with Brendan."

"What if he says no?" I asked as Doris wandered off.

"Good question." Ricardo tore a piece off his garlic bread. "Speaking of questions." He looked at Mia. "We've been wondering about the treasure."

I groaned. "You, too?"

Mia laughed. "You have to admit it's intriguing. The idea that there might be some fabulous treasure hidden in your house."

Gillian said, "The only problem with that theory is

that I've been through every cupboard, drawer, and box, looking for things Cass can sell online to make a little money to tide her over. Trust me, I haven't found any treasure worth speaking about. Some lovely old costume jewelry, but that's about it. Why does everyone think there's a treasure here?"

"My dad worked on a book about this house before he died. One of the things that intrigued him was the story that Doris' father had smuggled and hidden a treasure trove of jewels here that was never found." She gazed at Ricardo. "People are talking about it again with the latest murder."

"You think the murders on my beach are linked to the treasure?" That was an unsettling thought, but it explained the tips to the police.

Ricardo said, "I doubt it. Amelia was killed on the beach, right? I seriously doubt that there's a treasure chest buried there. So let's get back to the séance. I'm thinking me, Mia, you, Jack, Gillian, Doris, Samantha, Brendan."

"Should Brendan be there?" I asked, happy to change the subject. "And we invited Niles and Dave. I thought they could use the distraction."

"That'll be interesting," Ricardo said. "What about Mina and Professor Stone?"

"Don't you think we'd be playing with fire if we invited Darius? And I'm not sure Mina would come," I said. "I planned to start with the script I used last time but build in more time for any responses we get. Doris should be able to sense if anything supernatural is around. One ghost to another."

And the lights flickered and died, casting the room into overcast mid-day gloom. Hazy light seeped in through the windows, casting more of a pall than illumination.

"Jack, can you light the candles?" Two red pillar candles decorated the table. I could get the LED lanterns out, but it wasn't really that dark and the lights would come back on anytime.

Gillian laughed. "Ah, the perks of living in an old house with trees that shade the windows."

"Let's finish this delicious meal. We won't be able to reheat anything without power." I helped myself to another piece of garlic bread.

"There's a light on down the street." Jack looked out the window. "Just your power, sis."

Mia's phone screen lit up as she made a call. When someone answered, she put it on speakerphone. A familiar voice said, "Hello?"

"Hey, George, it's Mia. You're on speaker. I'm at Cass' with Ricardo, Jack, and Gillian. Power's out to the cottage, but neighbors have lights. I know it's not your job, but are there any power outages you know of? It's getting dark soon, and we'd like to figure out the problem before we leave."

"I'll be right there." The phone disconnected.

My mouth fell open. I wouldn't have called George that fast nor would I have expected him to come right over. "What the heck?"

Mia smiled. "Just promoting a little romance."

"Does everyone know?" I was shocked that so many people were getting involved in my non-existent love life.

Then she got serious. "You have neighbors, but you're somewhat isolated right here on the beach. The murder hasn't been solved. Suppose the cops are way off, and the killer is some maniac stalking you? I think we should close and lock doors and windows until George gets here."

Jack glanced around. "She has a point. We should figure out what we can arm ourselves with."

I understood Mia's reaction. She'd had a rough life with little stability. But Jack?

"Kitchen knives?" I said sarcastically. "No baseball bats, I'm afraid. Brooms."

"Pepper spray," Mia said, pulling her keys out of her backpack. A small pink container dangled from them.

I might feel safe here, but I needed to be more sensitive to her feelings. "I have black pepper in a can. Won't hurt him, but it would be unpleasant."

"Any Tabasco?" Ricardo asked. "Vinegar? Alcohol? You have a gas stove. Boil some water."

Gillian put the kettle on. "There's a hammer in the junk drawer."

"Good. Get it. We'll close and lock up together." Jack checked the kitchen windows.

Although I thought everyone was overreacting, I gave up, and we moved around the first floor together, locking up. Then we collected various weapons and armed ourselves.

"Notice how we've all assumed the power outage was intentional and not a transformer blowing somewhere in the vicinity." I jumped at the sound of the doorbell. We all moved over to the door together and held our weapons up as I opened it.

George raised an eyebrow and took a step back. "Oh, good. Five amateurs armed to the teeth with…vinegar? What could go wrong?"

I did feel foolish as we stepped aside so he could enter. "I thought I'd be happy to see you." I closed the door behind him.

George made a face "Did you call the electric company to see if there's an outage?"

"Did you notice the other lights on in the neighborhood?" I countered.

"Point taken. Yes."

"The security light and porch lights were out before the house lights went," Jack said.

"Hello, I'd like to know if there are any outages at 22 Blue Heron Court? No?"

We all whipped around at the sound of Mia's voice.

"Our house lights and the exterior safety lights went out. The neighbors seem to be unaffected… An hour? That would be great. Thanks." She pocketed her phone. "What? Somebody had to do it."

"Ever practical," Ricardo said. "Will they seriously be here in an hour? That never happens."

"Don't count on it happening," George said. "I'm calling this in and treating it with caution, given recent events in the area, until the cause of the outage is determined. All of you," he pointed, "Stay inside."

As he went out the back door, we moved into the living room. Maybe it was my imagination, but the shadows in the room seemed to be getting longer.

"Anyone want anything to drink before it gets warm?" Jack asked.

"Another beer," Ricardo said. "Mia?"

"Someone has to stay sober." She softened her comment with a smile.

"I'll finish putting the food away," I said as I

stacked plates.

"Cass, George told us to stay together. I think we should all move into the kitchen," Mia said.

The kitchen with its window facing the beach was much cheerier. Now that we were nearer the back door, I could hear voices outside. I lifted the corner of the curtain a bit until I could see George. He was talking to Niles as Bill Daniels walked up.

We huddled near the back door, listening.

"What's the situation?" Bill said.

George pointed toward Dave's house. "They have power. Cass' house doesn't. Two safety light bulbs are smashed. Power to the house is down."

A truck pulled up in front. Niles, Bill, and George hurried around to meet it.

"Let's go," I said and started out the front door.

Ricardo grabbed my upper arm. "Not without looking first." He opened the blinds.

The truck out in front was marked as the electric company. The police and Niles approached the burly repair guy.

"ID?" George said.

"Sure." He pulled a lanyard with a plastic badge from under his jacket.

I opened the door and stepped out onto the porch.

George scowled at me.

I ignored him. "Don't take this the wrong way, but I've never gotten service this fast anywhere I've ever lived."

The repair guy laughed and tucked his identification away. "I wanted to see your place. It's the end of my shift. I was leaving work and volunteered."

"Seriously?"

He shrugged. "Sure. I was hoping you'd give me a tour. We were all jealous of Bart when he got to come out to enhance your service. Your house is haunted, you know." He winked at me.

"So all I need to do to get great service is to mention that I have ghosts?"

George's head snapped around and he stared at me.

Rats. Screwed that one up. Then I thought about it. This couldn't be the first time George was hearing about my place being weird. Doris said the cops teased him about it. I narrowed my eyes. Did George think that I didn't know?

Niles watched George thoughtfully. I wondered why he'd come over here without Dave.

"Yeah, that'll work until we've all been out here." He grinned. "Now let's take a look."

"Anything I can do to help?" Niles asked.

"I think we're good. Thanks for your help." George smiled, dismissing Niles.

Niles nodded and headed off to Dave's place.

Bill and George caught up with the repairman as he checked connections. Ricardo, Mia, Jack, Gillian, and I returned to the kitchen where I finished putting the food away and loaded the dishwasher by the light from the window.

"The atmosphere's right to finish discussing the séance," I said. "But I think we need to keep it down. Did you see George react?"

"I noticed that," Jack said. "But didn't he know that séances had been held in your house?"

I nodded. "He did, and Doris said he'd been teased by the other cops. But I haven't introduced him to her, so he's only aware of the rumors. He's very," I looked around to make sure he was out of earshot, "superstitious."

Ricardo grimaced. "But you have to tell him sometime."

"Maybe," I said, but I knew he was right.

"Come on," he said. "You can't lie to the guy."

"No, I don't want to lie to him." Funny how having someone tell you to do something made you want to resist.

"Not a good thing to do in a relationship. Breaks trust."

"I know, Ricardo." I sighed. "But, hey, letting him know about Doris might drive him away."

At that, Doris appeared dressed in a gray and white seersucker shirtwaist dress with a matching fitted jacket. The hat perched on her dark bob bore a Navy insignia on the front.

"Where've you been and what are you wearing?" I looked her up and down.

Mia walked around her for a closer look. "Nice. Vintage. What? WAVES?"

Doris twirled to give us a better look. "It's the best of the women's uniforms, in my opinion. It's designer fashion. I'm ready for action." She squinted in what I assumed was supposed to be a steely-eyed look of readiness. "I've been keeping an eye on things to make sure you were a-okay. No stranger entered our house." And she saluted.

"I've always wondered," Gillian said. "What does WAVES stand for? I know WAC is Women's Army Corp."

"They had difficulty coming up with something nautical sounding," Doris said. "It stands for Women

Accepted for Volunteer Emergency Service."

"That's a stretch!" Ricardo said.

I laughed. "Thanks, Doris. Don't salute me. I should have known you'd be watching out for us. All this makes me realize that I need some indoor battery-operated lights in case the power goes out at night. Maybe a camera or two."

"That might be going too far," Ricardo said.

The lights came on.

"Yay!" I said.

Ricardo expelled a breath. "Okay, back to our purpose."

Doris faded. "Don't forget, I'm always here. If you want me to appear, call out."

"Thanks, Doris," I said.

"Before you go, are Bill and George still here?"

Doris' disembodied voice said, "They're still looking around. You should tell him about me."

I closed the dishwasher, wiped my hands, and put the towel down.

Gillian made a cup of tea. "I've been dying for this ever since the lights went out. Not to belabor the point, but you should make up your mind now. If we do the séance tomorrow night before we leave… George might not be happy if he finds out afterwards."

"If George finds out what afterwards?"

Chapter 16

We all jumped at the sound of George's voice. George and Bill had come in the front door while I clattered the dishes and we were talking in the kitchen.

"Pardon the intrusion. I assumed you'd want to know what we found," George said. "Are we interrupting something?"

"Not at all."

"The repairman reattached your cut wires. Yes, they were cut. The bulbs in your safety lights were shot out. While I'm pleased that you put up the caged ones, they're no match for pellets." He gripped my shoulder. "This was intentional. Is there something you want to tell me?"

"We didn't hear anything," I said, trying to shrug out of his grip. "I have no idea who'd want to do something like this."

"It's still close to Halloween. It could be teenagers, daring each other to pull a prank on the haunted house," Jack said.

Bill said, "Your neighbors didn't hear anything, either. You're not alone here tonight, are you?"

"Jack and Gillian are staying until Sunday." I was hoping George would volunteer, but Gillian spoke up.

"Jack and I have to leave on Sunday."

He nodded. "Jobs."

"Keep the doors and windows locked and call the

station if you even think you hear something. There's still a murderer out there," George said. "You could go to a motel or a B&B."

"We'll keep the place locked up," I said. "And I can't afford a B&B. Maybe the police department needs a web site?"

Bill snorted with laughter and tried to cover with a cough.

"We'll be going then." George stopped as if he were going to say something else but thought better of it and headed for the door.

"Thanks." I followed them to the door and locked it behind them as Doris reappeared.

"You knew they were coming in, didn't you?"

She nodded. "I heard them, but I knew you weren't ready for them to meet me."

"You should have warned us." I knew I was taking my anxiety out on her. Doris faded out, and I immediately regretted my tone. I turned to Ricardo and Mia. "It's all right if you guys want to leave." I was having a pity party, but I couldn't stop.

They exchanged a look, but Mia said. "No way. We have a séance to plan."

I was profoundly grateful for the additional company and hoped Doris would also forgive me. "Back to the table?"

Jack and Ricardo opened their laptops.

"Are you all right?" Mia asked.

"Not entirely." I smiled. "I'm a bit spooked. Why would anyone shoot out my lights with a pellet gun? Or cut my wires? I really want this murder solved. But I'll be fine. Thanks for asking." I thought back to Dave's proposed tour. Had he said something to someone who wanted to find that treasure? He said he needed money. Had Dave shot out my lights? Was he looking for the loot? He might want it, but despite his recent behavior, I couldn't believe he'd do this to me.

She nodded. "I don't know Mina, but she's spent her whole life here. If any one of us has a connection to this place, it's her. We don't know how far down her roots go. Her parents may have lived here when Doris was killed on the beach."

Doris eased back into our reality. "I'm going to go outside to see what I can see."

"Doris, I'm sorry."

She shook her head. "It's not what you said. I have a creepy feeling."

"Now I'm worried," Jack said. "What does it take to give a ghost a creepy feeling?"

"Go ahead, Doris," I said. "Let us know what you find. Mia, you're the tech brains. Any chance we're being spied on electronically?"

She shrugged. "There's always a possibility. Devices are small."

"Not on my computer," Ricardo said, but he picked up his phone and appeared to be taking pictures around the room. He spent more time with his camera focused on the archway leading into the kitchen.

Mia and I stayed still and quiet while Ricardo got up and walked into the kitchen, saying in an overly loud voice. "I'm getting a beer. Want anything?"

"Nothing for me," I said, watching him closely.

He opened the fridge door, grabbed a beer, and rejoined us. "I think we should have another look at your loft to see how much room we have available for the séance." His words were stiff and careful.

I took the hint. "Sounds like a good idea. Let's go." Once all five of us had cleared the stairs, Ricardo held his finger up to his lips. "Do not yell. Keep your voices low and monotone. I don't know how powerful the microphone is."

"What microphone?" Jack asked.

I shushed him.

"I have an app on my phone that detects possible spy cameras. It can get false positives from reflections, but it kept reacting to a fountain pen in your kitchen."

"I don't own a fountain pen. They used to leak on my fingers."

He grinned. "I didn't think so. You doodle with a pencil. I'm guessing it's a spy camera containing a microphone."

"Are you serious?" Jack demanded.

Ricardo shrugged. "You can buy one online for twenty bucks."

Mia nodded. "It could be sending a signal to someone or a receiver close by, but it's more likely to be a USB device. So it would be recording and could be retrieved and plugged into a computer for download later."

"I vote we dump it in a glass of water," Gillian said.

"I'm curious to see what it picked up. I'm calling George."

When he answered, I explained in a low monotone what was going on.

"Have you considered hiring a bodyguard?" He paused. "I'm joking, but you are really keeping us busy."

I wanted to say that I hoped he'd move in to protect

me, but I refrained. "I may have to if this keeps up or you guys will bill me for visits."

"Be there soon. Don't leave the house. Don't answer the door. Don't do anything."

"Yes, sir." I hung up.

"Let's go make sure the pen is still there and the doors and windows are locked. We can make small talk about the séance until George arrives. We have to plan it anyway."

I led the way back down, chattering about room size. Spy cameras! This situation—whatever it was—was getting pretty dicey. Someone she knew, someone who was still around, must have committed Amelia's murder. She hadn't been killed by a stranger or a transient.

And the murderer had access to my house.

George arrived quickly and didn't beat around the bush. He went straight for the pen and bagged it first in plastic then in a reflective pouch. "Did any of you touch it?"

We all shook our heads.

"Good." He sounded angry, but I was willing to bet he was worried about us. Then his face relaxed. "Look, I'm glad you called me. I don't think this has anything to do with you personally, Cass. It's more likely that someone, who's been in your house, knows that you and I are acquainted and wants some insight into what the police are doing. Could also be a treasure hunter or even be a reporter. Don't worry. The cut lines might have been a diversion to allow this to be planted. This is a lead that could prove useful."

"I'll bet Amelia knew her killer, and it's one of our suspects." I grimaced. "And I hope you're right that I'm not being targeted. I've felt really safe and happy here."

George raised an eyebrow. "*Our* suspects? Don't worry. We'll be keeping an eye on you." He shot me a lopsided grin. "I'll take this back to the lab. You all should try to relax. Lock the doors after me. Don't go outside alone after dark. I don't care what noises you hear. Do not answer your door unless you know for sure who's on the other side."

"Will do." I showed him out and returned to Ricardo and Mia. "You two were pretty quiet."

They exchanged a glance, and Mia said, "There wasn't much to say. Thinking that this all would be easier if you were straight with George."

"It's not too late." Gillian pursed her lips. "No? Okay then. Back to séance 101. What've we got?"

"Not much. Notes off the internet. My loft. And someone who wants answers."

"We have two people who want answers: Samantha and Darius." Ricardo opened his laptop. "Are we addressing both of their concerns? I think he should be included."

I lifted a shoulder. "Yeah. He's been miserable. We can at least try."

Ricardo made a few notes. "I have access to a couple of resources." He closed the laptop.

"Do I want to know?"

He laughed. "Probably not. We should go now. We'll check in with you tomorrow. I'll let you know what we find out."

"Guess we're really going to do this. Want your leftovers?"

"No, you keep them." Ricardo slipped his laptop into his backpack, slung it over his shoulder, and they headed out.

I locked the front door behind him and kept watch out the window until they started their car and backed out of my driveway. Ricardo turned on his headlights, and I realized that with the days shortening, dusk had sneaked up on us. I returned to the living room.

Gillian said, "I'm sorry we have to go in a couple of days. I feel really bad about leaving you here alone."

I shook my head. "Don't worry about it. I'll be fine. Really." I sounded more confident than I felt. "I have a couple of strapping neighbors to help."

"Let me remind you they're both suspects in a murder."

"Yeah. That pen narrows things down. It had to have been placed by someone I know who was in my house."

"It wasn't necessarily the murderer. Dave might have done it to find out about the treasure and remember Mina's offer of refuge."

"Under her stairs." I mock-shivered. "Spiders." But I had no expectation of having to use her dusty cellar for shelter. Jack reset the modem after the electrical outage knocked it out.

"Speaking of the outage, do you remember who showed up?"

"Niles?" I answered. "I thought it was a bit odd at the time."

"Could be a coincidence," Gillian said.

Doris floated in as I settled myself onto the couch. She'd returned to civilian clothes and wore a blood red midi with cap sleeves and a flowing skirt. "What's up?" She floated onto the armchair. "Nothing's moving outside except all the lovely little creatures that let me inhabit them as they scurry around the neighborhood. It took a while to get a ride back here. Seagulls are almost too dimwitted to influence. Too focused on fish." She made a face.

I imagined Doris trying to get a seagull to abandon fishing long enough to fly near my bungalow. "Do me a favor and keep an eye on anyone who comes into the house? Especially Niles. Someone will try to retrieve it, and I want to know who put that pen on my counter."

My cell rang. "It's George." I walked back into the kitchen. "Hey, George. What's up?"

"How're you doing?"

"I'm a little shaken, but I'm good. You must be calling for a reason."

"I had a question or two. We talked about possible treasure or loot from bygone eras at your cottage. Have you talked to anyone, aside from Dave, about a treasure or a cache of jewelry possibly located at your cottage? We know about him. But anyone else? It might be the motive for the person or persons harassing and spying on you."

"I had the same thought. Mina's books and local legends mean that quite a few people are aware of the rumors. To answer your question, no, it's not something I promote." I thought about Dave. "But Dave might have promoted the idea for a local legends tour. He wanted to bring people into my house and tell them about buried treasure. I said no. What brought this up?"

"Let's just say that it's a tangent we're investigating. It may be completely unrelated to the murder. We have a tip line and have to follow up."

I wondered what tip they'd received. "So someone said that the murders on the beach are related to a buried treasure at my house?"

"Something like that."

"How like that?"

He sighed. "The tip was that two groups are fighting over the treasure hidden by the smuggler. Hence the bodies. Allusions to treasure somewhere in or around your house keep coming in. It's probably that treasure rumors always capture the public imagination, but we have to follow up, so lock your doors."

"Yes, Mom." I hung up and returned to the living room.

Everyone stared at me, and I shook my head.

"I'll have to work on his manners. He never says goodbye."

"Mom?" Jack asked.

"Oh, he was fussing over locking the doors."

"And what about treasure hunters and murder?" Gillian asked.

"They got a tip—maybe more than one—and I got the impression the cops think the attacks on me have to do with someone's belief a treasure is hidden here. Doris, do you remember anything relevant either here," I pointed downward, "Or in the area?" I circled my index finger in the air.

"There've always been rumrunner rumors around. Y'know, burying the loot," Doris said. "And as you know, plenty of real rumrunners."

"But nothing about a treasure that you remember?"

"I remember plenty of 'get rich' talk, but nothing about a specific treasure."

"It bothers me that the rumors seem to be ramping up," I said.

"I be interested in the treasure. Arrgh," Jack joked

in a piratey twang.

I ignored him. Baby brothers. "Gillian and I went through nearly everything in this place. We found hair jewelry, an engagement ring, and some amazing costume jewelry."

Gillian nodded. "We found a few beautiful pieces that would have been considered costume jewelry in their day but were made with semi-precious gems. One necklace is cut amber and jet. But lovely as those pieces are, they don't constitute a treasure trove. Nothing that would have meant a fortune to a rumrunner."

"How does it tie into the murder?" Jack asked. "Unless… Do you think he heard something on the USB drive?"

I shrugged. "I doubt it. We didn't talk about it." Then a chill skittered down my spine. "But we did talk about Doris."

Chapter 17

Gillian gave me a pitying look. "You may have lost your chance to tell him yourself."

I sighed and dropped my head. "All right already. As soon as I can, I'll do it."

"Good! A treasure could be buried under the cottage," Gillian said.

"Or the garage," Jack added.

"I haven't found any secret panels or hidden—" I stopped. "Actually, that's not true. There are cupboards under the eaves."

"I used to play up there as a child when I came to visit my mother." Doris wavered in and out, a sign of her strong emotions.

I wanted to hug her, even knowing it would be impossible and I would feel the wet damp of her ghostly form.

"I'll stay down here and finish getting our news programs set back up." Jack picked up the remote.

"That's my honey, dodging the hard work." Gillian laughed. "Let's grab some cleaning supplies. There's bound to be dust."

"And spiders." I shivered.

We carried up dust cloths, cleaning spray, and a couple of bags. I expected spiders, dust, and the broken stuff people stash in corners and forget about, the detritus of their lives.

"I'll work on the area between the two window seats. Want to start on the other side?" I glanced at the moonbeams dancing along the tips of the low waves. "Suits me." Gillian turned on all the lamps. "If we don't finish by the time you want to go to bed, it won't be a problem if I we leave stuff out on the floor or window seats."

As we worked, Doris floated in and out. Sometimes she came up the stairs, but she often startled us by sticking her head up through the floor to check on our progress.

"I'll be lucky if she doesn't give me a heart attack." Gillian picked up a naked, broken china doll with one eye that wouldn't close, examined it, and tossed into the garbage bag, shaking her head.

"I heard that." Doris' disembodied voice echoed through the loft.

As I cleared the space, I tapped on the sides and bottom of each shelf. I removed drawers to see if anything was taped to the bottoms. After clearing four large drawers, I unpacked a box of clothes, put them away and broke the box down. "This treasure hunt could work to my advantage if I get some of my neglected unpacking done."

I had more storage space than I'd originally thought. The next section along that wall was a two-door, two-shelf cabinet. The top shelf looked empty, but the bottom shelf yielded three dolls, a pile of clothes, several porcelain dogs, and three children's books.

Doris instantly appeared. "Those are mine!"

"What? Do you have radar? How did you know I'd found these?"

"I came up to tell you George is here."

"Oh." I felt mollified. "Guess I'd better go down to greet him." I climbed down the circular staircase.

"I'll stay up here and keep working," Gillian said.

George knocked as I opened the door, startling him. "Hello. C'mon in." I stepped aside.

"X-ray vision?"

I laughed. "Funny you should say that. I…" I couldn't tell him the truth even though I'd started to. "I was about to take a break to get a drink. Gillian and I have been going through the storage areas in my loft. Would you like something to drink or eat?"

"I'd take some water."

"Coming up." I poured him a glass of water and grabbed a cream soda for myself.

"Hi, George." Jack said as he finished setting up the news for recording. "We're having catch-as-catch-can leftovers for dinner if you're hungry."

"No, thanks. I've eaten."

"Want to sit down here and let us in on what's going on or do you want to talk while we work upstairs? I sort of hate to quit now that I'm on a roll."

"I'll follow you up, but why are you cleaning at this late hour?"

I opened my mouth and closed it again.

His eyes narrowed at my hesitation.

"It's your fault. You got me all intrigued at the thought of buried treasure. I have unpacking to do, so I thought I'd clean out some cabinets, look to see if anything's hidden, and get my clothes out of boxes and into the built-in drawers upstairs."

"You've always been a little crazy." He followed me upstairs. "Hi, Gillian."

She stood and dusted off her hands. "Hi, George. Off work?"

He nodded. "Thought I'd stop by to try to keep you out of trouble."

I showed him what we'd done, and he opened and closed everything again and sat on the window seat.

"What did you find?"

"So far, it looks like stuff that would belong to a little girl."

George nodded. "A little girl did live here at one time."

"There've been quite a few owners, but I think these belonged to a little girl who visited her mother here while her father, her legal guardian, smuggled stuff." I didn't mention that the girl hadn't left the premises.

"Stuff." George shook his head and smiled. "I think you're wrong about the little girl living with her father. The information we have is that a writer named Shelagh Macalin lived here with her daughter Francine. Any toys probably belonged to Francine. In any case, that tallies with the information in our files and what I've been able to research, which you may have guessed is why I'm looking for hidden treasure."

I sat back on my heels. I'd forgotten about Doris' much younger half-sister. "Then do you want to tell us what we're supposed to be looking for specifically? A chest brimming with jewels? A fabulous necklace? Spanish bullion?"

He laughed, his eyes crinkling at the corners, and I saw my George for a few minutes. "We don't actually know. Given that we're talking about a smuggler, my guess would be gems. Could be cut or uncut. If they had originally been in jewelry, they would have been removed for two reasons: easier to transport stones and would be too recognizable in their original form. There are a lot of stories about this place and what went on here."

Jack joined us. "It was getting lonely down there."

"You can help me." Gillian went back to cleaning.

"That sounds like fun." Jack's monotone belied his words, but he picked up a dust rag and pitched in.

George looked around. "This place is supposed to be haunted."

I tensed and dodged the implied question. "I'm surprised you came back in that case."

"Do you believe in ghosts, Cass?"

I had the impression he was baiting me. He'd heard us on the flash drive. I was sure of it. "You know about Doris, don't you?"

"Is that what you call her? The little girl who owned these toys? I'm afraid I set you up when I mentioned Francine, and you hesitated. I now know that you've been holding out on me, and I'm wondering why."

My heart raced. "George, I—"

"Because of me." Doris stepped daintily through the wall, lifting her feet as if to step over an invisible threshold. She picked invisible lint off her very short flapper skirt. A band encircled her dark bob with one large feather rising straight up from the middle of her forehead. Her eye makeup exaggerated her eyes. She pouted and batted her eyelashes at George.

She'd taken the decision away from me, but I knew it was overdue.

His eyes narrowed, but he didn't move as she

173

advanced on him shimmying.

The fringe on the dress swung wildly. There was no sound either of footfalls or swishing fabric. She stopped in front of him. The top of her head barely reached his chin. She looked up at him and put a finger on his chest.

"Boo!"

I held my breath. Jack and Gillian appeared frozen in place.

George was the only person who'd met Doris that didn't look around for projectors. He was the only one who actually believed in ghosts before he saw her. I had no idea how this was going to go.

George licked his lips. "I'm George." He didn't take his eyes off her, but he put his hand into his pocket. He clearly wasn't about to offer to shake hers.

I suspected he already had an idea what shaking hands with a ghost would feel like. I remembered the green onions. Would he have some with him because it was Halloween season and spirits were about? Or because the other cops had told him that my house was haunted? He was the only person I knew who would expect to see a real ghost this time of year. He had come to my house prepared.

Doris curtseyed. "Pleased ta meetcha. We're going to get along just fine."

He didn't take his gaze off her, but he addressed me. "So your cottage really is haunted."

"Yes." I bit my lip.

He nodded. "Uh huh. Doris, what do you want?" His enunciation was clipped, precise.

Doris cocked her head. "To know why I'm still here." She narrowed her eyes at him. "Is this the old get-rid-of-the-evil-spirit-by-giving-it-what-it-wants routine?"

His eyes widened, but he continued to focus on her. "I'm not an evil spirit."

"That's what they all say."

Now that sounded more like George the cop to me. I hoped the shock of meeting Doris was wearing off. I took small, shallow breaths.

Doris turned toward me. "He hasn't run screaming yet."

I coughed before I found my voice. "No thanks to you." I tried to laugh, but it sounded more like a croak.

"If he's going to help us, he has to be ready for whatever happens during the séance. It's now or never. Either he loves you or he doesn't. Either you trust him or you don't!"

George cleared his throat. "Excuse me. Séance, Cass?"

"Yeah, Samantha wants to contact—" I waved my hands around.

Jack cut me off. "George, Darius wants to contact Amelia—"

Gillian talked over both of us. "We thought we could clear Darius and make Samantha feel better about being in love with Brendan."

"Really." He finally broke visual contact with Doris to look at Jack, me, and Gillian. "You two knew all about this?" He raised an eyebrow.

Jack nodded and looked down at the floor.

Gillian said, "Since last summer. We found out while we were helping her move in. I was terrified at first. But Doris…well…Doris is… Doris cares about Cass and helps protect her. She won't hurt you."

"She nearly gave me a coronary." Cautiously, he glanced back at Doris.

Doris put her hands on her shimmery hips. "I can be scarier."

"I'll bet you can."

"In my defense," Jack said. "I wanted Cass to be honest with you. She cares about you, and a relationship shouldn't be built on a lie."

George tapped my chin with his finger. "Your ghost is right. You should have told me."

"I was going to." There was that defensive tone in my voice again. "I was waiting for the right time."

"So I had to hear about her and your séance through someone else's spy media." Still watching Doris, George took a deep breath and cleared his throat. "I don't want you following me home."

There was the crux of it. "Doris can't follow you home."

George raised an eyebrow. "How do you know she can't follow me?"

"We don't know why, but she has limits." I wasn't sure I should tell him about her ability to possess Thor.

"So she says."

I opened my mouth to tell him more, but he held up a hand and said, "Later."

Doris shook her head. "You're thinking that maybe you shouldn't say your plans in front of me." She shook her head and her fringe danced. "You're a real pipperoo. Or in modern parlance, Dude, I can go invisible and listen in, anyway." She raised an eyebrow and leaned toward him.

He pulled back.

Her eyes narrowed and she smiled wickedly. From

my perspective, it looked like she'd just gotten the upper hand.

After a pause, he segued. "I'm off tonight."

I swear my heart skipped a few beats. "On call?"

"Nope." He waggled his eyebrows at me, and I laughed. He looked around the room. "I've never taken a close look at this room before."

"It's not like you've made a habit of coming up to my bedroom."

His eyes widened. "True." Then he turned back and pointed at the built-ins across the room. "The roof is pitched."

"Yes."

"Insulated?"

"Has to be or you'd be able to roast chicken in the summer and make ice cream in the winter."

"Sounds like someone's hungry." He laughed. "So, there's a triangular space between the tops of the cabinets and the roof all along there where they meet?" He traced a line with his arm from one end of the loft to the other.

Gillian picked up the used paper towels and threw them into a trash bag. "I'll carry this stuff down." A hint of a smile played across her lips as she looked at me and went downstairs. "C'mon, Jack."

I'd tapped the sides and bottom of each cabinet but hadn't considered the tops. "I don't know for sure. Let's look." I went to the cabinet I'd cleared out last and reached up. There was a flat top. "There'd be a triangular space above this one." I moved to the open top shelf of the built-in bookcase. "Not here. If you reach up, you feel a slanted top."

"So I'm guessing the roof was insulated and

finished on the inside with the material you see in your vaulted ceiling. Then the cabinets and drawers were probably built as units and put in place under the eaves; whereas, the bookshelves were built in place between the storage units. That would mean that there are areas behind and above the cabinets and drawers."

"You'll tear up my bedroom, won't you?"

He winced. "You're going to hate me all over again, aren't you?"

I sighed. "No, but I will grouse a lot. The only thing that will make this better is if you tell me what's going on."

"You could refuse."

"You'd get a warrant or at least try. We'd be at odds. When you finally got in, it would be a hostile takeover. No. I'm every bit as curious and interested as you are."

He looked around the room. "The Rumrunner Murders. Rumors abound. Loads of local stories. My guess is that you're being targeted by treasure hunters because the murder has brought up all the old stories again."

"Why hasn't this bungalow been searched before? It was unoccupied before I bought it."

"Who knows? Maybe it has."

I nodded.

"If we do a thorough search, regardless of whether we find the treasure or not, it should divert interest from your house as a possible treasure hunting site for the general public. You'd be safer afterward."

"I get it. I might not be a target of the current murderer. That does make me feel better." I smiled. "What's involved?"

"We'll move your things down for you. You should pack up anything personal. We'll wrap the bed in plastic." He paused, looked down, and back up. "We might have to remove some of your built-ins."

I looked around. "I love the window seats and built-ins. This is such a cozy space."

"Don't worry. We'll put it all back the way it is now."

"I bought this place as is. I own everything in the place. Do not throw away anything you find, and I want to see everything, and I mean everything that you find. Is that clear?"

He hesitated, and I narrowed my eyes at him. Then he nodded. "I will talk to my boss. To gain fast and willing access, I think what you're asking for is reasonable."

"If I get those assurances, we have a deal."

He held out a hand, and I shook it, enjoying its warmth and strength. At that moment, I wanted to pull him close and never let him go again. "It won't be as bad as you think. You'll be seeing a bit more of me."

"I can live with that." I smiled up into his warm brown eyes, sighed inside, and led the way downstairs.

Gillian and Jack were watching the news.

"Anything new?" I asked.

Jack leaned forward and paused the recording. "Not really. What's up?"

"I've given permission for them to search my loft."

Gillian frowned. "But not before the séance, right?"

I turned to George. "We're having a séance for Darius and Samantha tomorrow."

"Seriously? That fast?"

"C'mon, George. Jack already told you. They both want answers. Darius wants to know what happened to Amelia and…" I looked at Gillian and back at George. "I suspect to tell her that he still loves her."

George pursed his lips. "I don't really think that's a good idea. Do I need to remind you that he's a suspect in her murder? I could say that we need to start our search tomorrow."

It felt as though the temperature in the room dropped ten degrees. I put my hands on my hips and lifted my chin. "And I could say get a warrant."

George's eyes narrowed and his lips thinned.

For a moment I thought he would challenge me, but he let out a frustrated sigh.

"Still headstrong. You're playing with fire."

I stared him down and his body relaxed.

"Okay. Look, before we rip up your woodwork, I'll go down to the station in the morning. There's a piece of equipment that should make it possible to get some idea if there's anything in there, and I want to talk to my boss. Lock the door behind me."

He paused as if waiting for something, but I only nodded. He grabbed his jacket and left.

Chapter 18

I woke to the smell of coffee and got up. I wrapped my silk kimono around me and headed downstairs. "What time is it?" I stood in the kitchen archway.

"Good morning." Gillian brought me a steaming cup. "You slept pretty soundly."

I rubbed my eyes and took the coffee from her. What was it about coffee? "Ah." Plopping onto the couch, I tucked my feet under me and leaned my head against the back cushion. The smell of pungent cinnamon wafted to me.

Gillian placed a plate of morning buns fresh out of the oven on a trivet on the coffee table. A black paw surfaced from the other side of the table.

"Not for you, Thor. Come into the kitchen."

My furry black cat followed Gillian into the kitchen and emitted a cracked meow. A can top popped, followed by slurping noises.

Gillian returned. "That'll hold him for a while."

"Where's Jack?"

"On the beach. He thought he'd get a little time in with the sand and sea before we head home. He'll be back soon." She nodded toward the buns. "Try one."

I picked one up and smelled it. "Mmm. He's missing out." I ripped the bun apart, pulling the outer edge away, breaking off a piece, and taking a bite. "Oh, these are wonderful." Soft, warm, cinnamony, sweet.

Yum.

"Thanks. I made them."

"Gillian, you have unsuspected talents. You've been holding out on me."

She laughed. "It's all Jack's fault. He said we don't cook."

"I'm glad he insulted us." I raised the bun in a salute to her, took another bite, and then licked the warm frosting off my fingers.

"Thanks. More coffee?"

"Please."

After my second cup, I went upstairs to get dressed. When I came back down, Jack had returned and was helping himself to the buns.

"Morning, Jack. Why are you frowning?"

"It doesn't feel right leaving before we know you'll be safe."

Gillian handed him a cup of coffee. "We have to earn our living," she reminded him.

Someone rang my front door bell. I merely turned my head. It was a testament to how emotionally spent I was that I didn't jump out of my skin.

"Should I get it?"

"Yes, thanks, Gillian."

To her credit, she checked the peephole Jack installed. "It's Samantha." She opened the door. "Hi, Samantha. C'mon in. Would you like some coffee? A cinnamon bun?"

Today Samantha was dressed more simply than usual in a blue and silver bohemian outfit, the yoke over her amplitude emblazoned with embroidery and beads. Her wavy red hair hung loose down her back. She seemed relaxed as she walked over to the glider and sat down. "Yes, please. I'm glad you're all here. I've already told Ricardo. I love the web site, by the way."

Gillian brought her coffee. I pushed the plate of buns toward her. She closed her eyes, peaked her hands over her nose for a moment, opened her eyes, and took a bun from the plate. "Okay. Remember when I said I'd get back to you with details for a séance?"

"Yes," I said.

"I'm looking for my dead fiancé, Gwilym. He was killed on your beach years before you moved in, Cass. At first, I looked for him because I missed him and was lonely. Now I want to find him to ask him if…if it's all right if I move on with my life."

"I'd noticed that you haven't been back recently to film. I assumed you were still working on a new prototype camera."

"That's part of it, but after Brendan and I started dating, I got sidetracked. The police said they'd return my camera after the trial, so I let it go. Put it out of my mind. Focused on the here and now."

"Understandable."

"The 'now' circled around and brought me back to where I started. I know it might sound crazy, wanting Gwilym's permission, but it feels right to me. The time has come. I do think there's order in the universe and that it doesn't pay to disturb the order."

"I've wondered why you thought he was still here, haunting my beach."

"I don't know for sure that he is, but I really want to know what happened to him."

"You're looking for closure." I saw the shimmer behind Samantha and knew that Doris was sympathizing with her. "We'll do what we can to help you find it."

"Thanks, Cass. I know there are no guarantees, but I really feel I have to try. I've been doing a lot of research on what happens when we die. I couldn't bear the thought that he was just gone." She wiped her eyes.

"Does Brendan know you want to do this?" I asked.

"Yes, but I can't really tell what he thinks about the séance. He clams up."

My heart broke for her. "I'm not sure we're going to find the answers you want."

"I really need to try." She wiped her eyes and blew her nose.

"Okay then," I said. "I guess this séance is on. We'll do it tonight. I'll leave it up to you to tell Brendan."

Samantha nodded. "I'll figure something out." Samantha took a second bun.

My phone rang. "Hello? Oh, hi, George."

"How are you doing this morning? Still alive?"

"Ha ha. Yes, we're all alive. Maybe you scared the bad guys away. You should come by more often."

"I might just do that."

That stopped me. "Really?"

The air in the room felt as though it were vibrating.

"What was that? Did you feel that?" Samantha said, her voice rising as she looked around.

"What?" I said, momentarily distracted from the phone.

She waved her hands in the air. "It was as if all the little air molecules were dancing."

Yup. That was a pretty good description. Her

perspicacity surprised me.

I pursed my lips and shook my head. "Nope." I lied through my teeth.

"Maybe your furnace kicked on," Gillian said. "It does feel a little warmer in here."

I turned back to my call. "Sorry, George. Samantha's here."

"I won't keep you. We don't have anything new. I'll let you know if we discover anything germane, and I'll be by later to check your cabinetry."

"Nothing more on the pen?"

"Not yet. I'll check on you later. Bye." He clicked off.

I dropped my phone in my pocket. "No one's scaring me out of my house now that I know about a potential treasure here." I said half to myself.

"It's not worth dying over," Jack said.

"Treasure? Don't be hasty," Samantha said.

I laughed. "You all are welcome to stick around and help me look. It seems there's a rumor of hidden gems in my house, but I sure haven't found anything. I could use a little filthy lucre to pay my bills."

"Don't forget your friends if you find it. I have to go open the shop. Do you mind if I take another of these for the road?"

"I'll get something for you to put it in." Gillian went into the kitchen and returned with a metal sandwich box. "Here you go. Please return it when you're through with it. Glad you like them."

"Love them. Thanks for understanding and agreeing to the séance."

"Whatever we can do to help. I'm also curious about what will happen. See you tonight and please don't spread it around about possible riches."

"Of course not." She winked as she slipped out the door.

Chapter 19

"Doris," I said to the air.

Doris stuck her head out of the wall. "Ready to see what I can see?"

"Let's go up and find out before we have to set up for the séance. Gillian, can you put the food away? Doris and I are going to conduct a little experiment. If this works, it will save me a lot of grief."

"No problem. When you're through, I've finished all the linens in the house. With Doris' approval, you now have enough stock to set up a store on any of the swap sites, make a little extra money, and find homes for some of these lovely embroidered pieces."

"Works for me." I went upstairs. "Okay, Doris, see what you can find."

"All set."

While she wandered through the woodwork as only a ghost can, I took the flashlight from my bedside drawer and examined the bookshelves more carefully. The back section abutted the roof, and I couldn't see or feel anything directly above the top shelf. If something were behind the back wall, it would have to have been placed there before these cabinets were added. I wondered if they were original.

Doris popped out down by the ocean-side window seat. "I don't see anything but dust and dead bugs on the side with the windows."

"Are you looking above and behind the cabinetry?"

She nodded. "I'll do the other side now." She disappeared and reappeared almost immediately. "Is the roof pitch different on each side of the peak?"

"What?"

She steepled her two forearms together and then pushed one elbow out further. "Does the back half of the top roof go out further and shallower on the back side?"

I thought for a moment. "Yeah, I think it does. Why?"

"There's more room behind the built-ins on this side of the roof. It's low but someone could lie behind the shelves like a hidey-hole."

"Now that's very interesting. Sort of like a priest hole though this house isn't old enough for that."

"It's been used by someone."

"Recently?"

"Not as far as I can tell, but there're some old, musty blankets lying back there as if someone or something was back there. The space looks to run the length of the room." She shrugged her delicate shoulders. "Maybe it's nothing. Left over from when it was built. I don't remember being in there." She frowned. "I don't see how someone could get in there now. I used to play up here when I visited my mom. I told you. This was all here then." Her eyes grew distant. "Wait. That's not entirely true. I have a vague memory of them swinging outward. I don't remember the space because, as a child, I didn't understand it as a space behind the cabinets. Somehow these cabinets move." She dove through the built-ins.

She was back out a moment later. "The middle

cabinet. Open the doors."

I did. "Three drawers. That's different. All the others aren't covered by doors, and they have two drawers, not three. I didn't notice that before." I opened the top one and closed it. I tried to open the other two, but they didn't budge. I yanked. Nothing. I looked at Doris.

She nodded and smiled. "Open the top drawer and take a close look at the drawer facing on the inside."

I did as I was told.

The drawer facing was hollowed out and contained two levers. I pressed the one on the right, and a section of cupboard and one of drawers swung out and away from where I was kneeling. I pressed the one on the left and the same thing happened on the other side, revealing the space and the blankets Doris had referred to.

"That's clever. A hidey hole, indeed." Wrinkling my nose, I poked around, moving the blankets. "Those are disgusting. There's a finger hold here so that someone could crawl in and pull the structure into place. It would latch automatically, but it could be opened again from the inside. But I don't see any treasure in here. Rats. If it existed, this would be a great place to hide it. I wonder if the rumrunners stashed hooch up here?"

The doorbell rang.

"Must be George."

Doris stuck her head out the front of the house. "It's George."

"I should have saved the money for the peephole."

Doris grinned.

I went down.

Jack had already let George in. He handed Jack an envelope.

"You're street legal."

Jack whooped and took the paperwork over to the couch. Gillian scanned through news shows as she sorted through one of the remaining knick-knack boxes.

"We're good to go. Literally. As soon as she's insured."

"Doris will be thrilled."

George furrowed his brow but turned to me. "Now we can get a look behind your built-ins without ripping them up." He brandished a tool that looked like a short, electronic club or microphone.

"As to that, I have a surprise for you."

"What might that be?" George raised an eyebrow and followed me upstairs. He whistled when he saw the open cabinets. "You've been a busy girl."

"I hadn't opened all the drawers and doors before. I haven't been here long, and there were other, more pressing things that needed to be done. While you were gone, I opened a number of them, including this one." I indicated the open door on the middle cabinet that wasn't part of either moving section. "None of the others contains drawers behind doors or three instead of two drawers. The bottom two don't open, but the top one does." I pulled it out and pointed at the levers. "Have a look."

"Now that's clever." He knelt inside and traced wires and cords from the levers up and over to pins that held the two sections in place along the wall. "I always wanted to live in a house with secret passageways and hidden rooms."

"Seriously?" I'd never considered that George had

much of an imagination.

"Absolutely! I spent a lot of time reading when I was a kid. I love mysteries and ghost stories."

"There is no way you are going to convince me that you read anything supernatural. You're way too superstitious."

"It wasn't about the ghosts. It was about the mystery. Why they were killed. Solving the puzzles. The stories often took place in houses with secret passages that were revealed by following the ghosts. Like mysteries, the stories I read often ended up with solved murders and justice for the victims."

I shook my head. "I can't tell you how surprised I am."

George stood up after his examination of the mechanism. "You're brilliant!"

A cough echoed around the room.

I smiled. "I wish that were true, but I had help."

A pint-sized Doris walked through a built-in and stood in front of him.

"Now why didn't I think of that? You could really be handy in police work."

Doris put her hands on her hips. "Figure out a way for me to leave this property, and I'm happy to help the local constabulary."

George laughed. "So you do have limitations."

"I told you she couldn't follow you home."

He nodded. "Yes, you did. Good to know it's true. Did you find any treasure?"

"You arrived right after we found this, so Doris hasn't checked behind every unit yet. Do you see anything back there?"

He slipped off his jacket, picked up his flashlight

and the tool he'd brought with him, and crawled behind the built-ins.

His voice was muffled, but I thought I heard him complain about how small and filthy the space was. I smiled. He backed out and sneezed hard enough to startle me. "I'd suggest getting a garbage bag and throwing those blankets out."

I held up a trash bag, pulled the old rags out, trying not to shake loose any dust but checking for anything important, balled them up, and put them in the bag. "I'll have to open the windows and vacuum before we do the séance tonight."

"Can you vacuum now? We might as well clean these cubbies out while we've got this open."

I scrambled downstairs and carried my wand vacuum back up. "We'll have to dump the canister fairly often. It doesn't have the capacity a bag vac has, but it's small and runs for 15 minutes on a charge." I held up the recharging cord I'd brought up.

George spent the next fifteen minutes clearing out the spaces and then running his machine over the walls.

Doris whispered in my ear, "He's a keeper."

I nodded. I love a man who cleans.

"Find anything?" I asked when he emerged.

He set a plastic bag on the end of the bed. "Not what we were looking for but interesting nonetheless."

I poked the bag. "Keys, glasses, an inlaid cigarette holder—that's pretty."

"Do you smoke?"

"No, but it's pretty enough to display in a case. Let's see. Some coins. Wonder if they're worth anything? Oh, these are pretty." I held up a pair of what looked like delicate gold and moonstone chandelier earrings.

George examined them. "Those are beautiful, but they're not the treasure we're looking for. Looks like they're yours to keep."

"Works for me!" I tucked them into a teak jewelry box on my bedside table and went back to examining the bag. "A pencil stub, some scraps of paper, a couple of rocks. These nails are interesting."

"I think they're handmade."

"They're four-sided, not round. I'd like to keep those if they're not important to you."

He laughed. "Why? They're just nails."

"I know, but I've never seen a handmade nail before. I think they're neat."

George stood. "Looks like we won't have to rip out the woodwork, but it still begs the question about where the treasure might be if there is one. I'll get this back to the office and do the paperwork. Is the séance still on for tonight?"

"It is. Are you coming?"

His brow furrowed. "I won't know for a few hours yet. I will if I can."

I heard voices in the kitchen.

George glanced toward the stairs. "You are not supposed to be letting strangers in until we figure out who left the pen."

I smiled. "That's no stranger. I recognize Dave's voice."

We went downstairs and into the kitchen.

"Sorry, but you guys are a little late for breakfast."

"Dang." Dave snapped his fingers. "I knew I should have gotten here earlier." Then he grinned. "We thought we'd come over to check on you before the lawyer arrives and we sign legal papers." He stiffened as George entered the kitchen behind me.

For a moment he had seemed almost like his old, relaxed self. I wondered if the legal papers were about his defense or the trust.

George's face was inscrutable as he laid the bag on the table. "She seems to be dead set on having a séance tonight."

"Does that mean you'll be here for the séance?" Niles asked George.

"Will you two be coming?"

"Wouldn't miss it."

"You mentioned signing legal papers. Did the accountant arrive?" I asked.

Niles shook his head. "Not yet."

Dave looked at me, ignoring George. "He's not returning our calls. They go straight to voicemail. I'm a bit worried about him. He's overdue."

"I assume he's usually punctual?" George sounded skeptical. "I'd think it'd be a personality trait for an accountant."

"He's usually right on the money. Pardon the pun," Niles said.

"Let me know when he turns up. We have a few questions for him."

"Sure thing." But Niles didn't sound enthusiastic about calling him.

"You're all welcome to stay for lunch. It's nothing fancy. Just leftovers, fruit, and sandwich stuff." I pulled things out of the fridge and set them on the table.

Gillian put a stack of napkins and some plates down and got knives for the mustard and mayo. She took the bag off the table and set it on the counter near the back door where the pen had been.

Niles helped himself to sandwich fixings.

George touched my arm. "I'll finish up my search in the loft."

I made a cheese and sweet onion sandwich. Since I wasn't about to get kissed anytime soon, I might as well enjoy my favorite vegetable.

"It's not breakfast, but thanks for feeding us," Dave said and smiled at me.

"You're welcome, Dave. Anytime." Gillian passed him a plate of shortbread.

As we ate, I explained a bit more about what we were trying to achieve with the séance. Again, I was struck by the differences between Niles and Dave as we discussed Darius' and Samantha's need to experience their departed loved ones again. Dave accepted their beliefs and seemed eager to see Amelia. Niles, on the other hand, scoffed.

"You know, Niles, you don't have to come tonight if you have better things to do."

"Oh, no, I'm looking forward to the experience. Wouldn't miss it. Never been to a séance." He stood up. "Thanks for lunch. We'd better be getting back. Dave?"

"Cass, thanks. I'll see you tonight." Dave grabbed a couple of shortbread cookies and followed Niles out.

Gillian said, "Go on, Cass. I'll clean up."

I went back upstairs to George. "You don't think Niles will be a problem, do you?"

Chapter 20

"I'd love to be able to reassure you, Cass, but I think having most of the murder suspects at a séance in your bedroom is foolhardy at best."

George's comment jolted me back to Amelia's murder. I'd gotten caught up in the gem hunt and forgot that a woman died on my little stretch of beach. "I'm sorry. You're right. We need to focus on justice for Amelia."

George's voice was gentle when he spoke. "There is no we, Cass. Solving her murder is my job."

"And the treasure?"

The corner of his mouth quirked up. "Okay, hunting for it would be fun, but please don't put yourself in harm's way."

I smiled up at him. The corners of his deep brown eyes crinkled. "You betcha."

"Is that you betcha that you'll be careful or that you'll put yourself in harm's way?"

I laughed. "Wouldn't you like to know?"

He nodded. "Yes, actually I would."

Just to torment him, I said, "You could stick around tonight for the séance and find out."

He shook his head. "You're every bit as impossible as you were in college."

"What's that supposed to mean?" I put my hands on my hips.

"Never mind." His phone pinged with a text, and he read the screen. "I really have to get going, and you have some work to do in here before your guests arrive." He went down the stairs with a handful of more small stuff he'd found.

I followed him down.

"Where's the bag?" George checked around the kitchen."I set it on the table."

"I moved it over here." Gillian went to the counter. "It was right here." She pushed my doodle pad and pencils and the small bowl of paperclips. "I swear."

"I believe you," I said. "Don't worry we'll find it. George, I'll take those from you."

He dropped them into my cupped hands, and I laid them on the counter.

"Wait a minute." Jack waved the envelope George gave him earlier. "If you don't have anything you need me to do before the séance, Cass, I thought I could take him out for a spin."

"Insurance?" George checked the message on his phone again. "I don't suppose five minutes would hurt…if you're insured."

"The Internet is a wonderful thing. Already done."

"Go have fun while you can. I'll need your help later." I made a shooing motion.

"You don't need to tell me twice." Jack tapped George's shoulder, and they both headed out the front door.

I turned to Gillian. "I need a bit of time to think and make sure that I've got everything covered. I'm a bit nervous about tonight. There's a lot going on."

Gillian made herself another cup of coffee. "Now that I'm fortified, let's head up to the loft, finish cleaning up the mess we made, and get it ready for the séance."

I grabbed my notepad and a pencil. "And make notes about what needs to be done. A little organization will make me feel better."

Once in the loft, Gillian perched on the window seat and gazed down at the ocean. "The water is really blue today. Oh, my gosh!" She leaned forward.

Curious about what had caught her attention, I stood behind her and surveyed the scene over her shoulder. "Wow. I don't think I've ever seen Mina anywhere but her own house."

Gillian snorted. "Cass, you've only lived here a few months."

"True. I guess she has to leave her house sometime."

Mina walked along the beach in front of my house. She wore a long, diaphanous, pale lilac dress with a purple knit shawl around her shoulders. From our angle, I couldn't see her shoes. The wind caught her hair and blew it around her head. The ribbon she'd tied it with was helpless against the airy onslaught, but she made no attempt to curtail her curls.

"She looks young from this distance."

"True. You wouldn't know she was old by the way she moves." I squinted against the sun's reflection off the sand and water.

"It's really her clothes that make her look old-fashioned." Gillian leaned closer to the window. "Romantic."

"From a different age." I suddenly decided. "I'm going to ask her help with the séance. She used to attend them."

"Why don't you go down and try to catch her? I'll get to work up here."

"Thanks." I hurried down the circular stairs and out my back door, waving at Mina to catch her attention.

Mina saw me and raised her hand. She waited while I caught up with her.

"It's a gorgeous day for a walk. The sun and sea produce diamonds."

"So beautiful and part of the reason I love living here." I breathed deeply and decided to jump right in. "I'm having a séance. Would you be willing to help me?"

When I saw Mina from my window, she'd reminded me of a fairytale character. Up close and startled, she assumed the bird-like look I'd noticed when I'd first met her. She resembled a Great Blue Heron with her angular face and beak of a nose.

"Why me?"

"You used to attend the séances here, didn't you?"

She nodded.

"You could help me recreate the atmosphere and say the right words."

She tilted her head to the right. "Tonight."

"Yes. I'd be happy to provide dinner. Gillian is cleaning the loft right now. Please?"

She tried to suppress a smile. "I would only do this for you."

"Yes!" I fist-pumped. "Now I feel much better."

"I'll need to prepare." She wrapped her shawl closer around her.

"No problem. Anything you want."

"Your ghost." Mina shivered and looked toward the house.

She had been nervous the first time she visited my bungalow. "No, really. No problem. Doris is cool with it all now. I know she was very angry when she was called up, but she's…she's my friend now."

"She was terrifying when she appeared." Mina's shoulders rose.

I nodded. "I know. She and I went a few rounds before we came to understand each other."

Mina's shoulders dropped. "The séance itself should occur after dark. I'll gather my things and come down to your house." She turned to go and then paused. "How many people will be in your loft?"

"Let's see. You and me. Gillian and Jack. Ricardo and Mia. Samantha, Brendan, and Darius. Niles and Dave. Maybe George."

"So, a dozen people? That's a lot for your little loft."

"Yeah, it kind of grew. I hadn't intended for that many people to know. It's a long narrow space. I think there're too many of us for a circle. It'll be more of an oblong. Is that a problem?"

"There are a lot of myths about séances. It's more about atmosphere. Intent. Openness." She paused. "Desire."

I nodded. "Okay. We'll make it work."

She smiled and moved slowly away from me.

I watched her for a few minutes and went back inside. I grabbed a bottle of water and climbed the stairs to my aerie.

"Glad you're back." Gillian stood and arched her back to stretch. "Thought you saddled me with all the clean up."

I looked around. "Good job. Thanks for vacuuming

and breaking down those boxes. I'm going to have a lot to recycle this week. While talking to Mina, I realized that we'll have a dozen people here tonight if everyone shows up."

She whistled. "That's a lot. We should shove some of this stuff into your hidey-hole."

"Good idea." I opened the cabinet back up and placed a box inside. "We'll need to bring up cushions for people to sit on."

"Did you see Jack while you were downstairs?"

"No. He isn't back yet?" I shoved another box in the space.

"Haven't seen him or Doris."

"I didn't see Thor, either, so I'm guessing Doris has possessed Thor and is rodding around with the boys."

"Typical."

It took us another hour to finish up. We were downstairs sharing apple slices when Jack returned with Thoris.

"George?"

"Left in his car. Said he'd be back tonight. He has to check on the accountant or something. Are we ready for tonight? Oh, he said to give you this." He handed me an envelope and reached into the fridge and grabbed a beer.

"Not yet." I barely heard the gentle knock at the front door.

Jack answered it, and Mina stepped inside.

She set the quilted bags she carried on the floor by the hall tree, removed her long gray coat, and hung it up, revealing a gauzy lilac maxi. "Are you ready? Is the séance still in your loft?"

I looked upward reflexively. "Yes."

"This is a little prep work I need to handle before too many people arrive. May I go on up, please?"

I gestured toward the staircase. "Be my guest. Do you need any help?"

She shook her head. "Thank you, no." With the bags, she ascended without using the railing.

I was impressed.

I sat down at the dining room table and opened the envelope. Inside were a half dozen paper copies of photographs of a vase of odd flowers in the middle of a table. I flipped them over. On the back George had written: "You know flowers. Does this arrangement mean anything?"

Gillian asked, "What is it?"

Jack picked up the photos. "Looks like a scraggly bouquet."

"Odd choices for a bouquet." I kept staring at the bunch of flowers in a vase in the center of a dining room table. They had begun to wilt, but they were still identifiable. "Hang on a moment." I walked over to my bouquet on the mantel. A few more Stargazer lily petals lay on the floor. I picked them up. "These are poisonous to Thor. But they bloom in the spring. Why are they in this bouquet?"

"Hothouse?" Gillian asked.

"They'd have to be." I pointed to the photos. "Those blooms don't all grow in the same season, and I recognize several as deadly to cats. I wonder if they also affect humans?"

"I see where you're going," Jack said. "But I thought Amelia was hit over the head and had her throat slit?"

I frowned. "If Amelia bought them, it would be odd behavior. If someone sent them to her, it would be equally odd. Unless it was meant as a threat. These aren't blossoms you'd normally order from a florist."

Gillian shrugged. "If she didn't have pets, she wouldn't care. Probably wouldn't know. I wouldn't."

"Problem is she was staying at a rental for a few days. Why the posies at all?" I got out my guide to poisonous plants. "Let me check my suspicions." I flipped pages, comparing illustrations to the photo. "Foxglove is beautiful but can stop your heart. Monkshood, also called wolf's bane, is deadly. Columbine. A variety of lilies. And there are more." I looked up. "Guys, if I were a betting woman, I'd say someone sent Amelia a message."

"Apparently in a code she didn't get or didn't understand," Gillian said.

"But from someone who knew she'd be there," Jack added. "Who knew?"

"That narrows down the suspect list. No unknown attacker." I pursed my lips. "Dave. Niles. It might eliminate Darius. Gerry."

"Hold on a minute. Two things could be happening at the same time. She might have gotten this gift from an enemy. But separately she might have been killed by somebody who stood to gain." Jack flipped through the photos again. "I don't see anything else that stands out."

Gillian said, "It's getting late. We should get things ready down here. It's chilly and the wind has picked up. Jack and I should move our jackets to our bedroom so there's space on the rack for others. We have soda, beer, and iced tea in the fridge, but I'll have coffee and hot tea ready. I assume we don't want any food or drink upstairs."

"Probably a good idea. With so many people, there could be accidents that would distract us." I took my jacket and scarf off the hall tree. "If you don't mind, I'll put my stuff in your room, too."

"I'll flip on all the outdoor lights. When's George due?"

"I'm still not sure he's coming. Is your personal stuff out of the bathroom? Guests will have to use it."

"I'll check. Why don't you go up to see how Mina's doing?"

"Good idea." Mina had transformed the room. It no longer bore any resemblance to my bedroom nor did it look like the hastily thrown together stage set I'd been planning to erect.

"Wow, Mina. I like the indigo hangings over the windows, and is that a crystal ball?" I sniffed the air. "What's the smell?"

"That's a sage smudge. Instead of candles, I use diffusers for scent and controlled LED lighting. It's so lightweight to haul around and controllable. I can get a variety of hues and intensities to create the right mood. The ball focuses everyone's attention. I find that candles pull people away in different directions, dispelling energy."

"You just officially blew my mind. I so don't picture you and electronics. Cognitive dissonance."

Mina's laugh was high pitched with a fluting resonance. "Would it help if I told you that I prepared the crystal ball by boiling it in water and brandy for 15 minutes and drying it with a chamois?"

I nodded. "Yes, that actually does help."

"But it's a sinful waste of brandy. Is that two Ouija boards?" asked Jack.

"No. I left yours where you had it, but I brought along an automatic writing board with a pencil in the planchette. You never know what's going to happen. Several people could put fingers on the planchette. It might draw something instead of writing. Some artists say that automatic drawing is the source of some of their paintings. I also have a tape recorder as well as a digital voice recorder and an omnidirectional microphone. We might hear things later that were too subtle for us during the séance."

"So high tech." I shook my head. "I was expecting late night movie gypsy."

Mina's eyes crinkled at the corners. "I'm delighted not to be a stereotype." She placed a vase with a single blood-red rose on the low table. "But we also have to create a feast for the senses not only to relieve the anxieties of the participants but to lure any entities forward to engage with us." She set several tiny remotes on the table. "To control the various lights."

"I'm impressed. You've thought of everything. I'm so glad I asked you to help."

"The point isn't to control; it's to allow things to happen without barriers. I removed as many barriers as I could think of." She smiled. "You never know what will happen. That's the adventure." Her eyes sparkled.

Maybe I'd uncovered her secret passion. "I thought I was getting away from the drama when I moved here."

Mina's sweet smile gave her a knowing look. "Ah, Cass, I suspect you have only been asleep until now."

Chapter 21

I raised an eyebrow, not sure what she meant.

Now she looked around as if not seeing the walls of my loft. "There is something about this place. Not your house specifically, but this area about the bay. In many ways, it's an archetypal village. Perhaps small nature spirits peep out from behind the trees."

I could believe that. "There are local legends. We're planning to use some of the lore as a theme for our local business web sites."

"Have you researched local First People past and present?"

I shook my head.

Mina nodded and started to say something, but the sound of footsteps on the stairs cut her off.

Niles head popped up. "So this is where the magic happens."

Mina's eyes narrowed.

"We're not quite ready, Niles. I'll be right down," I said.

He didn't retreat right away but surveyed the space, taking his time. Then he slowly descended.

"If you don't mind, I'll stay up here." Mina stood up and dusted her hands off on her skirt. "Stairs get a bit difficult as you get older."

"I understand." Perhaps that was why I didn't see her out on the beach often. I climbed down and searched for Niles.

He sat on the couch and met my gaze as I scanned the room. Dave sat across from him in the glider, and there was the faint scent of sandalwood. "Hey."

I breathed deeply. "We're waiting for everyone else. In the meantime, did Gillian…?"

"I did." Gillian gestured toward their beer bottles.

"Okay then."

Doris' disembodied voice said, "Door." When I didn't move right away, she yelled, "Now."

"Gotcha."

"Let us in! It's cold out here."

I stepped back, and Ricardo entered followed by Mia, Samantha, Darius, and Brendan.

Brendan helped Samantha out of her coat and hung it on a hook. "Will we all fit?"

Gillian took Mia's black velvet cloak from her. "I'll put this back on the bed, okay?"

"I'll be back in a minute." Shivering, I headed out to my porch and called George.

"Hey. Séance can't have started yet if you're on the phone. Something happen?"

"Not yet but this has to be short. Two things. In the pictures you left for me, did you notice all the flowers in the arrangement were poisonous and many were out of season? Some of them have to be from a greenhouse somewhere and special ordered. Also, do any of the suspects have an alibi?"

"Funny you should ask. Things aren't as cut and dried—pardon the joke—in real life as they are in a TV show. These are single males without wives or girlfriends. Their alibis are all loosey goosey."

"Technical term?"

He laughed. "We don't know about Gerry because he's still…"

I heard a lot of background noise that I couldn't make out.

"Well, speak of the devil. We got him. He's in Tijuana. Gotta go." He hung up.

I hurried back inside, happy to be out of the cold.

Darius, the only one wearing a hat, put it up on the very top of the old hall tree. "It's going to be a bit of a tight fit, but so many of us need some answers and it-it feels right to be together."

I returned his smile. "It'll work. Don't worry. Mina's upstairs and ready whenever we are. Let's head up to the loft."

Niles and Dave took final swigs and set their bottles on the coffee table.

Gillian turned out all the lights downstairs except the one in the bathroom at the end of the hall in case someone needed to use it. I led the way.

Upstairs I counted heads. Eleven people. A bit of a tight squeeze, and George wasn't here yet. I still hoped he'd show and tell me about Gerry. Gillian settled near the open stairway to prevent anyone from tumbling down. I nodded to Mina. It was her show now.

Mina sat cross-legged on a large, black cushion. The contrast with her pale lilac dress turned her ghostly. "Please find a seat in the circle. I've set up microphones and recorders. We may catch something that's inaudible during the séance. Occasionally, speeding up or slowing down the recordings finds hidden voices. If we do hear something later, we'll let you all know."

Niles whispered something to Dave that sounded like "Paul is dead."

Facing the stairs, I parked myself on the opposite side of the circle from Gillian. It gave me the willies to sit with my back to a hole or a door, always had. A remnant of childhood fears.

As people moved around her, Mina picked up one of the small remotes and pressed a button. The lights lowered. She lifted another, pointed and pressed. The gentle scent of sweet oranges wafted through the room. Couples sat together. Mina was positioned with her back to the windowless wall while Samantha and Brendan were opposite her. Gillian, Samantha, Mina, and I represented the points of a compass. Samantha leaned forward and placed a small picture of a man I presumed to be Gwilym on the table.

When everyone settled down, Mina raised the electric candlelight as Gillian turned off the room light. A very faint glow limned the circle where the spiral staircase opened to the floor below.

"Cell phones off or muted. If your cell phone is not in a pocket or purse, please place it screen down so as not to provide a distraction. The physical world can wait. We are now engaging with the spiritual world. Relax your bodies and minds."

Thoris padded up through the hole in the floor. I wondered if Doris had made her own circuit of the first floor before inhabiting Thor and joining us.

"You all are here to attend a séance. As Teilhard de Chardin said: 'We are not human beings having a spiritual experience; we are spiritual beings having a human experience.'"

A wave of energy swept through the room.

"The word séance means meeting. We are meeting here with a purpose tonight: to facilitate meetings between those in this world and those now beyond. Samantha and Gwilym. Darius and Amelia."

Mina's repetition of the word 'meeting' let me see the séance as less spooky woo-woo and more practical problem solving. Thor shook himself, took a clumsy step, and sat down to groom. I guessed Doris had left him momentarily. The front door opened, and I heard steps below. I started to rise, but Gillian shook her head at me.

Mina looked toward me. "I believe we have a latecomer. We'll resume in a moment."

Gillian remained seated but leaned over the opening and whispered, "Up here."

A moment later George appeared, looking a bit ghostly as he emerged from the hole in the semi-darkness. "Sorry." He sat down next to Gillian and nodded at me.

"We've set the table before us to be welcoming. While we are open to other communications, we would like to reach Gwilym first." Mina took a deep breath. "There are so many of us we won't hold hands during the séance, but let's begin by putting our hands on the table or floor to touch as best as we can little finger to little finger to establish a group bond as I call out to Gwilym."

We all stretched our hands, fingers spread, and tried to touch.

"Gwilym, we are here to communicate with you. Samantha has a question she would like to ask. If you are present, please make yourself known."

We sat in silence for a moment or two. A few people withdrew their hands or shifted. Someone whispered.

Mina looked at me and then at Samantha. She reached over and placed her fingers on the Ouija planchette. I was too far away. Samantha hesitated a second and then added her fingertips.

"Gwilym, I've missed you every day since you-you died. I've looked for you everywhere. Sometimes I think I see you on the beach." Samantha cleared her throat. "I'd like your blessing to move on." She glanced at Brendan. "I've brought Brendan with me. We'd like to get married…" She faltered.

Mina said, "Gwilym, if you're here, please give us a sign."

The planchette moved slowly and erratically over the board. It neither spelled anything nor selected yes or no. Then the pointer stopped and didn't move again. The automatic writing board was too far for Samantha to reach easily. Niles set his fingers on it, and Dave followed suit. After a moment, Ricardo did the same. The planchette moved hesitantly, but instead of writing, it drew a rough ghost in a cartoon style. The lighting made it hard to see expression clearly, but it appeared as though Ricardo glared at Niles, who clapped his hand over his mouth. His shoulders shook. Ricardo pulled the board away from Niles and pushed it toward Samantha, but she ignored it.

Mina took control again, removing a scarf from the crystal ball. It was a mesmerizing piece, and I found myself staring into the orb almost against my will. Samantha leaned closer. A cool breeze swept through the room. Mia gasped. I held my breath and listened.

Then Niles turned toward Dave and whispered, "Woo-oo-oo." He turned his laugh into a cough.

Samantha sobbed as Brendan's arm encircled her.

Thor crept up behind me. I caught the black-on-black movement behind the others and the glint of amber eyes. He softly pawed my back as he stretched to get close to my ear.

"Do you want me to bite Niles to shut him up or should I manifest as a hazy ghost and scare the heck out of him?"

Thoris was back. I wanted to tell her to fly at Niles and scratch his eyes out, but that wouldn't do any of us any good. Stupid man couldn't hold his liquor. "No. We can't rescue the situation," I whispered over my shoulder. "But if he gets too obnoxious, I give you my permission to sink your claws into him." I could have sworn Thoris snickered.

Mina straightened. "If any earthly participants would like to leave, now would be the time. Otherwise, I expect respectful silence."

Niles settled down.

Mina waited until there was dead silence. "Gwilym, if you're here and able, please give Samantha a clear sign that she will understand."

Samantha gasped and her eyes widened. "Thank you!"

I hadn't seen anything change. The planchette was still. I saw nothing in the crystal. No candles had flickered. And yet something had happened. She'd gotten her confirmation.

Mina seemed to sense it as well and changed gears as she read the road ahead. "Thank you, Gwilym." Another moment of silence although this one smacked of respect while the other a silence imposed by a head librarian. "Amelia."

Darius sat between Samantha and me but close

enough that I could see him stiffen at the sound of her name.

"Amelia, if you're here, please give us a sign."

I swear I saw the battery-operated candles flare, but that was impossible.

"Thank you, dear."

So Mina had seen it, too.

Darius reached a hand out. "Amelia." His voice broke. "Amelia."

Thoris pawed my back again. "She's here."

"I love you, Amelia."

A pop of light filled the room and faded immediately on a sob so fast I wondered if I'd imagined it.

"And she's gone," Thoris whispered.

"Where'd she go?"

"Into the light. That really pisses me off. Why does she get to go into the light?" Thoris stalked stiff-legged toward the stairs and disappeared down them. An eerie meow-howl echoed back up toward us.

"What the hell was that?" Niles said and stood up.

Mina's gentle voice reached out across the room. "Amelia is at peace now. She's gone into the light."

"You're telling me Aunt Amelia was here? This is some sort of trick." Niles, still standing, shivered. "What was that? A flash-bang?"

But I was watching Darius, and he smiled.

Mina closed her eyes and held both hands out, palms up. "Thank you for joining us here tonight. Spirits, go in peace. Peace and blessings on all who've attended tonight." Mina picked up a remote and raised the light level in the loft. We'd been dismissed.

Niles pulled his phone out of his pocket and looked

at it. "I have to get to the hospital."

But as he advanced toward the stairs, George rose and barred his path. "Don't you want to know who killed your aunt?"

Dave jumped up. "You know who did it?"

"I believe Cass has figured it out, and if she has, she should tell you. She was key to solving the murder."

"Thanks, Detective. As sad as it makes me to know who killed her, I'm happy that we'll have justice for Amelia." I turned to Darius. "That was clever of you to confirm the juxtaposition of Dave's house to mine at the Halloween party. That alone didn't tip your hand, but you should have resisted the temptation to send her that bouquet. I didn't suspect you until I saw those flowers."

Dave glanced at Darius and frowned. "Uncle Darius?"

Niles sat back down. "What flowers?"

Everyone looked toward Darius, who raised his chin. "I have no idea what you're talking about."

George picked up a photograph from the floor where he'd been sitting and tossed it into the center of the room. It landed next to the crystal ball. "I see prison in your future."

The photo was the shot of the vase of flowers. People exchanged glances.

"Foxglove is digitalis. Monkshood is aconite. This bouquet is a message. Every flower is poisonous to one degree or another. These flowers had to be special ordered because many are out of season. Notice that they are cut. Even touching some of these without gloves would bring on symptoms." I looked up at

George. "You got the autopsy report, didn't you?"

George nodded. "Amelia was poisoned. She died slowly and painfully. She would have been vomiting, cramping, and very weak at the end. Her killer watched her suffer and prevented her from calling 911."

Dave inhaled sharply.

"Darius didn't love her. He hated her. His fragile ego couldn't take her rejection. He's a cold man who wanted cold revenge." I shook my head. "I was so wrong about you."

Samantha and Brendan quickly scooted away from him.

"You shouldn't make claims without proof. You could be sued for slander." Darius' voice was very soft but venomous.

"All the potential suspects had insubstantial alibis. Three out of four had monetary gain, but only you had had the kind of relationship with Amelia that would warrant sending a bouquet."

"So sending a gift is a crime now?"

"Sending a poisonous one is murder. Only you had a motive of passion."

"The autopsy revealed her stomach contents," George said. "You fed her a salad that contained leaves from several of the plants in the bouquet and tea that contained enough digitalis to stop her heart." He turned to Niles. "That's why you were a suspect, Niles. You had motive and access to digitalis. We got the blood analysis before the complete autopsy report told us the delivery method."

I continued. "You set Dave up by using his scuba diving knife to deliver a blow to Amelia's head. A love tap? And sliced her throat."

"She was barely alive when you hit her. We wondered how you got her onto the beach. She's a small woman. Alive but stunned, you could have folded her into a large suitcase. We got hold of the owners of the cottage. They had a digital doorbell with a concealed camera. They kindly checked it for us and sent us this." George dropped a photo of Darius wheeling away a duffle-style suitcase large enough to conceal the body of a small woman on top of the other picture.

A muscle in Darius' jaw twitched. "I intended to reconcile with her and spend the night. All that photo proves is that she wouldn't take me back."

George nodded as if he'd been expecting that response. "The last nail in your coffin is Gerry Waverley."

Darius blanched.

"You should advise your henchmen not to flee to Tijuana if they don't speak Spanish. Also let them know the US has an extradition treaty with Mexico. I got the impression he was happy to see the police. He's terrified of you."

Darius' lips thinned to a line. "If you are intent on prosecuting me for something I clearly didn't do, I'd like to talk to my lawyer."

"No problem." George pulled out handcuffs.

"Those are hardly necessary." Darius pushed himself up off the floor.

"I'll be the judge of that."

People scrambled out of George's way as he advanced on Darius, cuffed him, and led him over to the stairwell.

"Bill."

A voice rose from below. "Here."

"Package is on its way to you." George guided Darius down to Bill's waiting arms. George turned back to us. "Thank you all for your assistance. Carry on."

"Let's give them a moment or two to leave. Gillian?" I caught her eye.

She nodded and went down, followed by Jack. A few minutes later she called up. "All clear."

"Okay, everyone. Thanks for your participation. Be careful on the stairs."

Mina sat quietly as the others gathered their things and descended to the living room. "Go on down. I'll smudge again before I leave."

"Thanks. I appreciate your doing this."

She nodded. "I enjoyed it. It's always good when a soul passes on." She winked. "And thanks for the additional excitement. I believe the balance in our community has been restored."

Thinking about Darius, George, and Mina's last words, I joined the others.

Chapter 22

I checked to see who was still here. Ricardo and Mia held each other on the couch. Gillian emerged from the kitchen. Brendan helped Samantha into her coat.

"Brendan and Samantha, you guys are welcome to stay if you want to be around people or talk about what just happened."

Brendan slipped on his jacket. "We're shocked and tired." He smiled at Samantha. "But we got the answer we needed. I find it very hard to believe that Darius killed Amelia." He shook his head. "We really liked him. I welcomed him into my home."

"I understand. I liked him, too, and was positive he was innocent. But someone reminded me of my own feelings toward my ex, and I realized just how deep the resentment can run. Still, I'm not sure I would have figured it out if he hadn't sent the flowers." I exhaled sharply. "You go on. We can talk later." I saw Brendan and Samantha out. That left Jack, Gillian, Ricardo, Mia, Mina, and myself.

Mina came down the stairs, carrying her two bags. She set the large one by the hall tree and lugged the smaller one into the living room. "Could I have some tea, please?"

"Of course," Gillian said. A few moments later she emerged with a tray containing a teapot, mugs, bowl of tea bags, cream, and sugar.

"That was fast," I said.

"Hey, I'm good. Coffee's brewing, too. I'll bring munchies. I have a feeling it's going to be a long night."

Mina extracted her own tea bag out of a pocket, dropped it in a mug, and poured hot water over it. She settled into a large brown leather armchair by a small plant stand I used as a table. A ceramic lamp with a golden mica shade cast a warm glow over her. She withdrew a small laptop from a quilted bag and downloaded data from the digital recorder. After several minutes, she dug a small butter pat dish and a dainty silver teaspoon out of her bag and set them next to her mug. She dipped the spoon into the mug and lifted the tea bag out, placing it on the small dish.

Watching, fascinated, I wondered if she always came this prepared. So much for judging people by their appearances. I'd felt protective of Darius, and he turned out to be a ruthless killer. I'd assumed Mina knew nothing of the high tech world when she simply lived the way she wanted to, enjoying the elegance of a bygone era and incorporating the parts of the digital age she needed.

Mina looked up, saw me looking at her, and smiled back. "We'll have digital data in a moment. I have speakers for the tape recorder. We can listen to playback tonight, but I'll have to take it home to complete my analysis."

"Look at you. All high tech. Where did you learn all this?" I accepted the mug of coffee Gillian offered me. "Thanks."

"In a way, it's your ghost's fault."

"Excuse me?" Now we were seven as Doris

materialized in her seafoam green dress.

If Doris' intent had been to discomfit Mina, she failed.

"Doris, dear, now that I know your story, you are more friend than foe. Yes, your first appearance at that long ago séance led me to pursue this interest in determining if ghosts are real and how to interact with them."

Jack grabbed a beer and moved over to the dining room table. He opened his laptop and typed.

Mina set up small speakers for the recorder.

Gillian carried out sandwiches, crackers and cheese, hummus and pita, and fruit and set it all on the coffee table along with small paper plates. She selected half a tuna sandwich and poured herself some tea.

I pulled a dining room chair over by Mina and picked up a pad and pencil. She pressed play. The recorder picked up more from its position toward the middle of the loft than I'd heard back by my bed. I clearly heard Dave whisper "Knock it off" to Niles when he was acting out. Good for him. I heard Samantha's gasp. The pop I'd heard with the flash of light sounded like an old-style flash bulb exploding. The sob was clear but not entirely human.

Mina took her own notes. "I'm going to play this back for a few seconds. Listen closely and tell me what you hear." She hit play.

I might have heard a voice, but it wasn't clear. I shook my head.

Mia said, "It sounded like 'he killed me' to me."

Ricardo nodded.

Mina raised a hand. "She didn't say who. Listen again."

I still couldn't make out the words, but there was some sound that was barely audible. Jack paused his typing to listen. Ricardo leaned forward.

Mina opened the laptop and set it on her lap. "Give me a minute to find the same spot in the app."

The sound was clearer in some ways but also different. The tonal quality of the sob was different. I'd been thinking of it as a sob, but it was more of a sigh, like a change in air pressure. When the recording finished, I sat back and let the tension of listening intently flow out of me.

Mina looked around at us. "Did anyone hear anything interesting?"

Mia said, "The murderer was a man."

Jack said, "That lets you off the hook, Cass."

I stuck my tongue out at him.

Mina closed her laptop.

"Mina, what do you do now with the recordings?"

She reached over and patted my hand. "Before you attribute too much technical knowledge to me, I'll let you in on my secret: Maya and Theda."

"Our neighbors?"

"The very same. Tomorrow I'll take these recordings over, and they'll analyze them for us. They took me through what I needed to do for tonight with the digital recorder. I've used a tape recorder for years."

"Huh. Skills they learned in film school, I'm guessing."

She nodded. "There are other devices they suggested, but I didn't think you wanted a bunch of flashing lights and beeping."

"You're right about that." I sat back in the chair. "Okay, guys. What do you think?"

Gillian leaned forward, her elbows on her knees. "We all knew that ghosts existed before tonight."

Doris materialized in the middle of the sandwiches as Ricardo reached for one. He jerked back.

"Thanks for the demo, Doris, now can you let Ricardo eat?" I said.

She flounced out of the food. "Are you interested in what I observed?"

Gillian nodded. "Of course."

"Amelia was looking at Darius."

"I didn't see Amelia."

"Whether or not you saw her, she was there and then she was gone."

Mina yawned. "It's time for me to leave you all. It's late, and I'm tired. Maya and Theda will do their magic, and we may find out more but it will be tomorrow." She slipped the small laptop and little bowl into her bag and rose slowly.

"I'll see you to the door. Thank you so much for your help. I look forward to hearing what Theda and Maya find out." I walked her to the door, helped her with her things, and let her out. I kept watching until she'd made it safely back to her house and then turned back to the room, shutting the door behind me. "Anything else or should we call it a night?"

"I think we're still digesting what happened," Ricardo said as he and Mia exchanged a glance. Ricardo stretched and yawned. "Let us know what you find out."

"I'm glad the killer is going to jail." Gillian got up. "I'll get your cloak." She returned in a moment with Mia's velvet cloak. "Got everything?"

"We're good. Thanks again. We can show

ourselves out."

I turned to Jack. "As for me, I'm angry. What made him think he had the right to kill her?"

He shook his head. "Why does anyone think they have the right to kill another human being?"

"I'll help you clear up." Gillian picked up the plates to clear the table.

As I loaded the dishwasher, Doris materialized on the counter next to me with her head down. "It's nice to be part of the group. To not have to hide all the time."

"Were you lonely?"

"A bit. It's hard to be invisible."

"What about the breeze during the séance? Do you know what caused it?"

She shrugged. "I didn't feel anything."

Gillian set a stack of small plates on the counter. "That's the last of it." Gillian slipped some of them into the soapy water.

"We're going to bed," Jack said, taking Gillian's hand. "See you in the morning."

I rinsed the last dish off and placed it in the rack. "I'd better get some sleep, too." I turned out the lights and climbed the steps up to bed.

Chapter 23

My hands under my head, I lay in bed the next morning, staring up at the ceiling, thinking about the séance and its implications. I'd never given a lot of thought to what happens to us after we die. My family was nominally religious. Phil had zero interest. But my experience with Amelia left me wondering.

The sound of the sea sifted through the window and added rhythm to my thoughts, bringing some order to the chaos.

What had Samantha felt in the breeze that assured her Gwilym approved of her upcoming marriage to Brendan? Did I really hear a voice on the tape?

I rolled out of bed, gathered my clothes and toiletries, and headed down to take a shower. I really needed a second bathroom, but where?

Under the hot water massage, I washed away the pain of yesterday's revelations. No one tapped on the door, so I assumed Jack and Gillian still slept. When I shut the waterfall down, voices in the kitchen and the smell of coffee let me know I'd been mistaken. Throwing on my clothes, I only towel dried my hair. Big mistake. George was there, chatting with Jack and sipping coffee. I knew I looked like a drowned rat.

George smiled at me. "You look cute in ringlets."

My heart skipped a beat.

Gillian flipped a blueberry pancake onto a stack

and handed the plate to George, who took one and passed it to Jack. "Butter's on the table." Gillian turned to me. "Thought we'd give you a little break on our last day here. Have a seat."

I did as I was told. Jack handed me the pancakes, and I selected one and poured pure maple syrup on it.

Gillian opened the oven and pulled out a tray of sausages. "And for the meat lovers." She set it on the iron trivet.

Jack immediately speared two. "Sit down, sweet pea. Eat."

I touched my hair self-consciously. "Forgive me, George, but what are you doing here?"

He checked his phone. "Nothing so far. Darius lawyered up, but we put together a pretty good case. Thanks for your help."

"You're welcome." I bit into my pancake. "Did you find the greenhouse and confirm the order?"

"We did. Don't worry. Our case is solid. I'll be very careful what flowers I put in bouquets I bring you."

"I look forward to receiving any you choose to give me." I gazed into his lovely brown eyes.

Jack coughed. "We'll be heading back after breakfast. Work tomorrow."

"It's been fun having you all here for Halloween…despite the body. There is one thing I should clear up just so you know everything." I turned to George. "You've met Doris—"

George arched an eyebrow. "You really have a way of putting me on my guard. What about your ghost?"

"Remember when I said she had limitations?"

"Yes." He drew the word out.

I winced. "She can possess animals, birds, and insects."

"So she could follow me home."

"She thinks you're cute."

"Not making it better."

I sighed. "I don't want to keep any more secrets from you. She possessed Thor and spied on you at the police station." I ducked.

"You sent a ghost to spy on me?" Outrage and laughter mingled in his voice.

"Sort of. Remember when Jack came by about the car?"

"And brought your cat on a leash."

Jack froze. "You won't hold that against me, will you?"

Doris materialized slowly.

George tensed. "We need to come to an understanding."

She solidified and went all hands on hips. "What kind of understanding?" Doris batted her eyes and shook her head. Long, tasseled earrings swung wildly.

"Definitely not that kind." George looked at me. "Now that I know your super power, I want to set some limitations on your interactions with me."

"For example?"

"Do not enter my house unbidden."

Doris nodded. "I can agree to that. Anything else?"

"Not right now, but I'm sure I'll think of something."

Jack cleared his throat. "Don't get all depressed, Sis, but we're heading back to Berkeley now. We'll grab our bags."

"Come here you." I hugged him and Gillian.

"Come back any time."

George's phone dinged. "I'm heading out, too. Thanks for breakfast." He left by the back door.

Gillian said, "We'll come back for a weekend or two, but we were also thinking ahead to Thanksgiving. You have a much bigger oven, and I want turkey."

"Great idea!" I helped them carry their stuff to their car and waved goodbye.

Back in the house, I threw the linens in the wash and packed away the rest of the bedding. I sat down at the computer, pulled my phone out, and plugged it in to charge while I worked. The photos started downloading automatically.

"I'll send some of these to Jack and Gillian."

Doris leaned over my shoulder. "I really like that one of George."

Maybe I'd put that one in a frame. Maybe by my bed.

****

After lunch the house was desperately still. Usually the sea could lure me out and calm me with its whispers, but I felt hollow and listless. I sighed, and Doris materialized, smiling at me. I gave her half of one in return.

She tilted her head, arms akimbo. "What? I'm not good enough for you?"

"You know better than that."

"Down in the dumps?"

I nodded. "George left so abruptly and hasn't called or come by."

"What? It's been a couple of hours. Got a bit of a stick up his—"

"Doris!"

She shrugged. "I'll give you a choice: call George and confess your undying love or finish cleaning up your loft." Doris shot up through the floor.

The choice was obvious to me and apparently also to Doris. I wasn't dying to clean up, but finding the space behind the built-ins in the eaves meant that I could bring up some of the bedding from the bedroom downstairs and tuck it away in that space.

I unlatched the cabinets, swung them outward, and set the LED lantern from the side of my bed into the space, flooding it with light. Starting at the far end, I scrubbed the walls and floor and the tops of some of the cabinets, letting Doris' chatter about her childhood memories of her mother and this house wash over me.

My fingers touched something on a shadowy ledge. I jerked my hand back, afraid I'd uncovered a nest of spiders. I picked up the lantern and directed it to a piece of quarter round on the top of a cabinet. Lifting the light so that it shone into the area, I saw a row of large stones.

"Doris, I found something." I sat back on my heels.

Doris surged forward. I felt her slick coldness as she hovered next to me. "Those are my stones. My treasure."

Her reaction surprised me. "This is what George is looking for? *Your* treasure?" I wondered if a child's stories had sparked the rumors.

"I don't know about that. I found them when I was playing in here. They were in a bag. Some had a reddish tinge and some green. They reminded me of Christmas."

I took one and rubbed it. It did look a bit greenish. I scooped them all out and carried them into the bedroom. The dim, hazy sunlight seeping in was insufficient, so I turned on the lamp. "Hey. They changed color."

"Yeah. Red and green."

"No, I mean the stone changed from red to green."

Doris nodded. "Yes, I know. That's why I liked them. They were magical."

"You knew the secret all along." I sat back on my heels. "I have to take these to George."

I dug a clutch purse out of a drawer and stuffed the stones into it. I grabbed my keys and drove over to the police station.

I found George sitting at his desk. "Still neat as a pin, I see." I plopped down in the chair. "Hey."

He raised an eyebrow. "Have a seat."

I opened the bag and dumped the contents on his desk.

"Hey! You're messing up my desk with a bunch of dirty rocks."

"Take a closer look."

"What am I supposed to see?"

"The treasure."

He scoffed. "You've lost it."

"Nope. I've been working on the web site for Crystalline, a gem and crystal shop. Clean one of these off, check out the color in here, and then go outside and compare what you see."

George did as he was told. When he returned, he said, "Okay, they change color like a mood ring. So?"

I laughed. "So if I'm right, this is alexandrite. It's rare. It was discovered in the Urals in the 1860s and named after the Czar. I think these are the real deal. The lab-created stones weren't developed until the 1960s. If these were hidden in my house by the smuggler in the Twenties, they could be worth a small fortune. Up to $70,000 a caret. Not Bill Gates rich, but worth a tidy sum."

George sat up straight and glanced from me to the gems. "You may have solved another mystery." He picked up a pencil and poked at them with the eraser. "We'll have to get them checked out by a gemologist." He searched for a large manila envelope in his right drawer and pushed them into it without touching them. "Any more?"

"There might be." I shrugged. "There could be more up there under the eaves."

"Are you trying to lure me back to your house?" George's eyes narrowed but he smiled. "I'll give you a receipt for these."

"Does that mean I'll get them back?"

"Possibly. Probably, given the case."

"I love the way you never hedge."

He smiled. "Go home. I'll come by as soon as I can. At least with the murderer corralled, now I know you'll be safe. Thanks for your help."

"No problem. See you later." I left the station and drove home.

I entered my house, a little sad that Jack and Gillian had gone home. I closed the door, hung up my sweater, and tossed my keys on the counter. Then I saw him and tensed. Niles sat at my trestle table, drinking one of Jack's beers.

"Not cool, Niles! When people don't answer their door, you should go back home and call."

"Dave told me how he paid the taxes on this place using his proceeds from the trust." His words slurred together.

I kept quiet and waited.

"Technically, he has a claim on this place." He tipped the bottle, finishing it.

"You might want to ask Dave if he feels that way."

Niles slammed the bottle hard on the table. "He spent trust money paying those taxes. I'm a beneficiary, and he did that without my permission."

"I suggest you take that up with your lawyer." I fought against my voice shaking.

"Dave told me there's a treasure here."

"He told me that, too. It's a local legend. You are aware that most myths aren't true, right?"

He ignored my question. "Where is it?"

"Where is what?"

He nodded. "Uh huh. I'm not leaving any money on the table."

He was bigger and much stronger than I was but unarmed. I wondered if I could get away from him, but he was between me and the door.

"I gave everything I found to George." A pop of light and sparkles behind him. Doris! My rush of hope faded as I realized that she couldn't hurt him.

"You idiot! Why would you give a fortune to a cop? You had it free and clear. You could have been rich."

"No, because you're trying to steal it from me. Besides, they were looking for them for a case. Keeping them is withholding evidence." I backed up. "Why are you and Dave so desperate for money all of a sudden? You have the fund."

"I found out how much Gerry embezzled from us. That's why the weasel hightailed it to Mexico. We don't know if we'll ever get it back. I need that money. I'm in hock up to my eyeballs for student loans, and Dave will finally have to get a job."

I spun around as a car pulled into the driveway.

Doris reared up in full scary ghost mode and passed through us both. I'd never been so happy to feel her disgusting clammy coldness. Niles screamed and backed into me. The rear door and front door flew open at the same time as George and a uniformed cop rushed us. Niles and I both spasmed from a Taser shot. I felt as though I'd tangled with an electric eel and lost. The next thing I remembered was George holding me and checking my pulse.

I gazed up at him. "How did you know I was in trouble?"

George looked puzzled. "You sent me a text."

"No, I didn't." I frowned and regretted it immediately. My head ached and throbbed.

"Take it easy." He helped me up.

The cop snapped cuffs on Niles and led him out.

George showed me his phone. "Here." *George help niles atak home*.

"I left my phone on the charger. Haven't touched it since then."

"I have the evidence right here."

"Doris!"

She appeared.

"You sent a text to George."

George's eyes narrowed. "How does a ghost send a text?"

Doris vanished, and a moment later 'hi' appeared on George's cell from mine.

I held up my hands. "Look, Ma, no phone."

"You have one talented ghost."

Her laughter echoed around the room.

"Will Niles and Dave get the money back that Gerry embezzled?" I asked.

"We're working on it. He diverted dividends and stashed them offshore. We'll never know for sure what tipped Amelia Stone off. She couldn't get hold of Dave right away, but Niles was pretty pissed that the trust had been raided because he wanted to ask Stone for money to pay off his student loans. Apparently, he's always been upset that Dave was the principal beneficiary. He feels that Dave isn't honorable because he doesn't work and gets a free ride. Oh, and Gerry was Darius' source of information about Amelia. We're still sorting through the details."

Someone knocked on my back door. George let Dave in.

"Hey."

"Hey yourself. Are you okay, Dave?"

He smiled his lopsided grin. "I was about to ask you the same thing." Dave pursed his lips. "I wanted to talk to you about Niles. I talked to the cop outside."

"He said you told him about paying the taxes and that I owed you guys money. He was pretty angry. I thought he might attack me. Then somebody tazed me instead." I glared at George.

"Are you pressing charges against Niles? He's really upset. He wouldn't have hurt you." Dave sighed. "It's my fault that he even knew about the treasure. My stupid legends tour idea. I'm sorry. I'll get him to drop the lawsuit."

"What lawsuit?"

"He's desperate. He thinks you found something."

"I did. George has the stones I found."

Dave shoved his hands in his pockets. "Look, I don't know what's going to happen. But if you found treasure in the house, the ownership could be in dispute. You bought the house lock, stock, and barrel, so they're probably yours." He hesitated. "I've lost so much with Aunt Amelia's death. If he goes to jail, that would be the end of his medical career. He's worked so hard for so long. What was he thinking?" Dave slumped and looked away. "I think of you as family." He shrugged. "So I thought that even if I have any right to any of it because of paying the taxes, I'd like to let my share go so that you can stay next door and use the money to get the business going."

"Aw, Dave. I feel the same way about you."

George said, "I hate to break this up, but if it helps, Dave, she never thought you could kill your aunt."

"Thank you for believing in me. I'll really miss her. Didn't see her much, but she was kinda like a mom to me."

"There are lots of people who care about you. Like Doris' half-sister Francine. You looked out for her interests when she had no one else. Y'know, if either of us gets our hands on that money, we should see that some of it goes to her care."

"Niles was always the good kid, played by the rules, did as he was told. They'd send him to look for me when I went missing, and I frequently did." Dave's face softened as if he were remembering something long ago. "He always had to make sure I got to school safely. See that I didn't wander off on the way. He was the responsible one. I didn't know he felt so desperate about the student loans." Dave shook his head. "But all that will change if you press charges."

"George?"

He shrugged. "Up to you. Was this an argument among friends? Or was he trying to rob you?"

"I think it was just a misunderstanding."

Dave hugged me until I squeaked.

A word from the author…

I currently live in Cape May County in New Jersey after spending years in the San Francisco Bay Area with my Maine Coon cats Sierra and Ginger.

I attended Clarion Writers Workshop for Science Fiction and Fantasy at Michigan State University and sold a story I wrote there to Damon Knight for The Clarion Awards anthology.

I wrote technical manuals in Silicon Valley and also published several poems and science articles as well as a couple of chapters in Research & Professional Resources in Children's Literature: "Piecing a Patchwork Quilt."

I've also taught English in high school and community colleges.

Website: http://www.renaleith.com
Facebook: authorrenaleith

Thank you for purchasing
this publication of The Wild Rose Press, Inc.

For questions or more information
contact us at
info@thewildrosepress.com.

The Wild Rose Press, Inc.
www.thewildrosepress.com

To visit with authors of
The Wild Rose Press, Inc.
join our yahoo loop at
http://groups.yahoo.com/group/thewildrosepress/